CRITICAL ACCLAIM FOR WALTER KIRN'S
SHE NEEDED ME

"*SHE NEEDED ME* is winningly unpredictable. . . . Kim and Weaver may be among life's losers, but they've been given some awfully good lines. . . ."
                                        —*The Wall Street Journal*

"Kirn's followers will recognize . . . the same deadpan voice and dead-on vision that characterized Kirn's 1990 story collection, *My Hard Bargain*. But this time Kirn manages to skewer—or maybe barbecue—even larger chunks of the modern American dream. . . . Kirn and his sympathetic portrait of contemporary confusion deserve a warm welcome. We need them."
                                        —*People*

"Kirn allows us our whole range of feelings, conflicted though they may be. . . . Kirn writes toward complication and truth, rather than away from it, and wins me over entirely. . . . I, as reader, wanted to give myself up to a novel that would leave me, finally, unmercifully wrenched or unsurpassingly joyful. That *SHE NEEDED ME* refuses to do either is, while frustrating, quite possibly a measure of the novel's own truthfulness, and therefore, of its ultimate artistic success."
                                        —*Los Angeles Times*

"[An] entertaining comic novel. In Weaver's heady, heart-warming journey . . . Kirn captures both the comedy and the psychoses of the right wing."
                                        —*Washington Post Book World*

A BOOK-OF-THE-MONTH CLUB SELECTION

"A novel of subtle redemption and open-ended searching. . . . Kirn is at his best, crafting a strong woman coming to realization. Indeed, it is in character depiction that Kirn's talent breaks through. Drawn with devastatingly quick brushes, the characters' lives are revealed in broken lines, allowing the reader to fill in, without realizing it, the broken lines of people we all know. . . . There are times when Kirn shatters with a sentence. In the end, SHE NEEDED ME is an honest and illuminating portrait of two people lost."

—*Richmond Times Dispatch*

"SHE NEEDED ME oscillates artfully between religious satire and romantic sincerity. . . ."

—*Entertainment Weekly*

"A gentle, bare-boned but clever 'New American Regionalist' Midwestern novel. . . . I'm a bit ashamed to like Kirn's novel so much. I didn't think I could possibly sympathize with his protagonist. . . . But Kirn, a savvy, skillful novelist, crafts him into a sympathetic, even likeable fellow. . . ."

—*Philadelphia City Paper*

"If you want to read a modern love story, with a great plot and simple language effectively dealing with abortion, religion, and self-discovery, you most certainly should read this book. Walter Kirn dives headfirst into the issues of the '90s with SHE NEEDED ME. . . ."

—*The Muse*

"Walter Kirn is a cocky first-time novelist. . . . SHE NEEDED ME is like one of those artificial logs that burn with a sinister greenish flame: domesticated napalm. . . ."

—*Bookpage*

"I found one of the deep and lasting pleasures of SHE NEEDED ME to be a return to a writer whose voice taps into the sounds we all share, a lingua franca of our cultural life. It is a reliable, truthful, and direct way of speaking that Kirn manages to show us still exists; its meters are not without a hard, simple beauty. . . . Kirn also has an uncanny ear for the heartbreaking absurdities of his parents' generation, and his own. . . . And from this unclean pool of real moral life Walter Kirn enters again into the province that gives him his natural voice and power."

—*Newsday*

"Kirn's first novel is magnetically readable, told simply but not simplemindedly. . . . Chock-full of affecting and funny, affecting and creepy, and just plain affecting mundane incidents, and gingerly skirting sentimentality by means of strong characterization and an astringently ambiguous last page, this tale of two youngsters drifting in life and love might be the surprise hit first novel of the season."

—*Booklist*

"Intense. . . . Mr. Kirn is a writer in firm grasp of descriptive powers. . . . His sentences possess an unadorned clarity. . . . A dark and loopy journey."

—*Dallas Morning News*

"Kirn sensitively portrays his main characters' painful emotional waltz, perfectly capturing the hesitancy and mistrust that sabotages their yearning. . . . SHE NEEDED ME focuses more on the hearts of its protagonists, touching the reader's heart along the way. . . ."

—*Library Journal*

Also by Walter Kirn

My Hard Bargain

Most Washington Square Press Books are available at special quantity discounts for bulk purchases for sales promotions, premiums or fund raising. Special books or book excerpts can also be created to fit specific needs.

For details write the office of the Vice President of Special Markets, Pocket Books, 1230 Avenue of the Americas, New York, New York 10020.

SHE NEEDED ME

A NOVEL BY

WALTER KIRN

WASHINGTON SQUARE PRESS
PUBLISHED BY POCKET BOOKS

New York   London   Toronto   Sydney   Tokyo   Singapore

The sale of this book without its cover is unauthorized. If you purchased this book without a cover, you should be aware that it was reported to the publisher as "unsold and destroyed." Neither the author nor the publisher has received payment for the sale of this "stripped book."

This book is a work of fiction. Names, characters, places, and incidents are either products of the author's imagination or are used fictitiously. Any resemblance to actual events or locales or persons, living or dead, is entirely coincidental.

A Washington Square Press Publication of
POCKET BOOKS, a division of Simon & Schuster Inc.
1230 Avenue of the Americas, New York, NY 10020

Copyright © 1992 by Walter Kirn

All rights reserved, including the right to reproduce this book or portions thereof in any form whatsoever. For information address Pocket Books, 1230 Avenue of the Americas, New York, NY 10020

Kirn, Walter, 1962–
    She needed me : a novel / by Walter Kirn.
        p.   cm.
    ISBN 0-671-78093-X
    I. Title.
PS3561.I746S48   1992
813'.54—dc20   92-15909
                                     CIP

First Washington Square Press trade paperback printing October 1993

10 9 8 7 6 5 4 3 2 1

WASHINGTON SQUARE PRESS and colophon are registered trademarks of Simon & Schuster Inc.

Cover design by John Gall
Cover art by Terry Widener

Printed in the U.S.A.

For Deborah Bull, without whom this book might have been possible, but not probable.

With special thanks to Steve and Jamie Potenberg,
Judith Regan, the people of the Owl,
Jim Harrison, and Thomas McGuane.

SHE NEEDED ME

One

WE MET OUTSIDE AN ABORTION CLINIC.

The girl was standing up, about to walk inside.

I was in front of her, lying down.

I had gone there with some friends from church. The Conscience Squad, we called ourselves. Our leader was a man named Lucas Boone, a veteran of the Navy SEALs who had given his soul to the Lord of Hosts during an arctic training exercise. He said his conversion had something to do with the northern lights—their resemblance to the walls of a cathedral. That, and three weeks without sleep or hot food. What he learned up there, he told us, is that there are limits to self-reliance. Mastering hostile environments won't save you. Metabolic self-control is just another form of sinful pride. Kneeling before the aurora borealis, he laid down his pack on the ice and snow and was washed in the Blood of the Lamb.

Lucas's genius was planning and tactics. He picked the targets, the times. He drove the school bus. Surprise and nonviolence, those were the keys. The counterprotesters hated him because of his clever decoy actions. Lured by a phony memo or an anonymous tip, they would charge off to another city, sometimes a whole other state, while the Conscience Squad descended on a clinic just blocks away from their headquarters. A call from a pay phone along our route would alert the television stations, giving them just enough time to send cameras before the real action got under way. The press had a bias against us, Lucas knew, but it was outweighed by their need for quotes and pictures.

"Bloodsuckers," he said. "And I'm the blood."

Lucas understood the media.

As members of the Conscience Squad, we kept ourselves in a constant state of readiness, sleeping lightly, shoes beside our beds. We never knew when the call would come. A few of us, myself included, had lost good jobs because of this, not even having time to call in sick as we hustled into our clothes and out the door. On mornings when the school bus came, minutes mattered, excuses could wait. Lucas would honk the horn once, that's all; a second honk could rouse the neighbors, any of whom might warn the other side. If a person wanted breakfast, the school bus carried tea and doughnuts. Sometimes, on long trips, Lucas stopped at Burger King and ordered us malts and Whoppers. Myself, I was usually too wound up to eat.

My job was distributing the literature—snipping the twine on the heavy bales of pamphlets and passing them around to members before we reached the target clinic. The slicker handouts, the ones with color photos showing the disturbing, bloody truth of what our opponents called "the procedure," were obtained from a national clearinghouse in Georgia. The tracts that were made up of Bible verses and quotes from remorseful abortionists we produced ourselves.

For its boldness and disciplined organization, the Conscience Squad had received citations from public figures too numerous to name, including a Catholic archbishop and a U.S. senator. It was the first group I had been a part of that actually stood for something, some idea. There were rumors that even the governor supported us, although his advisers would not let him say so, for fear of offending liberal special interests.

I was very proud to be a member.

Things were running smoothly the day I met the girl. The clinic had only two entrances—in front for the patients, in back for the staff—the sort of simple layout Lucas dreamed of. I was stationed in back, between the Dumpsters and the parking lot. At Lucas's request, I had worn a suit and tie to contrast with some of the other members' clothes. A mixture of formal and casual outfits got the point across on TV that our membership had a range of backgrounds. A few of us dressed like 1960s hippies, and once were. Some of us were leading businessmen. We had women, far more than our critics acknowledged, and half a dozen blacks and Hispanics, all of whom were glad to stand out front and prove to the public our group was not racist. Most of us, however, were like me: ordinary caring Americans willing to do whatever it might take to put an end to child-slaughter.

By the time the clinic opened at nine, there had been scuffles, but nothing unexpected. As usual, the nurses were the worst. They loitered in the parking lot until their whole shift had arrived, then marched as a group toward the door. We didn't try to block their way, just stood in two parallel rows of nine or ten, praying out loud in unison and holding up our signs: UNBORN BUT NOT FORGOTTEN; EVERYONE DESERVES A BIRTHDAY; BE A HERO, SAVE A WHALE—SAVE A BABY, GO TO JAIL. The nurses reached our human corridor and started to spit and curse, the old routine. We smiled and did not react, our own routine. The nurses had almost reached the building when one of them, tall and broad-shouldered, older than the rest, suddenly stopped short and rushed my row, head down, claws out, wailing like a beast. We opened ranks and she shot right through, then recovered her balance and climbed on one man's back. Lucas's rule was clear: Fight if attacked, but defensively, never to do harm. The man whom the nurse was on top of—a lawyer friend named Derek Griff who did a lot of pro bono for the cause—ducked and backed up and let her tumble over him, and then, when she got up again, full-nelsoned her and walked her to the door. Fortunately for the nurse, the police had not yet arrived on the scene, or Lucas would have insisted she be held.

The patients—we didn't call them that; they were being maimed, not healed; we called them the mothers, the lost—began showing up about ten minutes later. By this time there were dozens of policemen and a K-9 unit, the usual government overkill, and all three news vans were parked and ready, antennas and satellite dishes raised to capture every nuance of the conflict. A ragtag group of counterprotesters, most of them students from local St.

Paul colleges, was milling around the edge of the parking lot, offering to escort the mothers in or if they preferred, to drive them to another clinic. When I noticed a group of them pushing my way, I took it as a signal to lie down.

Here is how Lucas had trained me to do it: First, I took a series of deep breaths and cleared my mind of fear. Then I pictured my body as a rug, a mat. I knew that some of the people would walk right over me. They might even kick me, driving their heels in, aiming for my genitals. What I was meant to do then was—nothing. Nothing but pray for them, calmly but audibly, letting them hear my concern and my resolve. Depending on the municipality, the police might drag me away at this point, or they might stand aside, uninvolved, scratching the ears of their panting German shepherds. Bruises were part of it, breathing was part of it. Mostly, though, it was Love.

Above me, as the group came nearer, I could see outstretched arms, a forest of them, holding out paperback Bibles and leaflets, waving them, showing the photos. The arms drew back as the group pushed on: Never touch the mother. I saw two boom mikes the size of baseball bats swing across the sky and hover there. I could hear Lucas preaching on a bullhorn. Sirens. The opposition, chanting. You could go off at such times, you could lose yourself. Better to stay focused, though. Alert. As the first of the line-crossers tried to step over me, corduroy trousers and bulky hiking boots, I called down a blessing on all of us: "Let live!"

The mother—a girl in her early twenties who had on a pair of tight black jeans and tennis shoes bursting out at the sides, the sort of girl you see in a store aisle and can't help suspecting of shoplifting cigarettes—stopped a foot away from me, stopped cold. There were men on either side of her, pro-abortion people, trying to move her along. She didn't budge. Such moments of dawning awareness and remorse were what we hoped and prayed for, the reason we rose before dawn, gave money, and worked whole nights in the chapel basement mimeographing letters to congressmen. But you had to be quick or they'd lose that glimmer, whatever it was in them waking up to save them.

"I'll help you," I said. "There are counselors here. They'll let you know your options."

The girl looked right and left, at the men, then down at me, arms crossed. Her brownish blond hair fell into her face. She tossed it back. "Stand up," she said. "I want you to stand up."

One of the men said, "He's crazy. Ignore him," and gripped the girl's wrist. She shook him off. A boom mike swung down and clipped the man's head. He slapped it away in a red-faced rage. Someone screamed—a cameraman, I think—and there was a sound of crashing glass and metal. Expensive, high-tech breakage. Everyone but the mother turned to look. Her eyes were fixed on mine. "You said you'd help me."

"Our counselors—" I raised my hand, a shield. It was a fight now, people were running. I thought I had glass in my eye.

"You," the girl said. "You said you would."

She crouched and held out her hand. I took it, panicking. A TV sound man staggered sideways into us, bleeding from his headset. The girl, falling backward, grabbed hold of my tie; I hooked her armpit, lifted. I glimpsed a clear path through the crowd and went for it, dragging the girl along by the elbow, amazed at how slim and light her body felt. People were screaming: "Fascists! Nazis!" People were screaming: "Baby killers!" A woman whom I did not recognize as belonging to either side was stooped in the parking lot in front of us, brushing the dirt off a trampled Bible.

Out of harm's way, behind some parked cars, I asked the girl if she was okay.

She touched her left earlobe, which was bleeding slightly. "I think I maybe lost an earring."

A police car nosed past: revolving blue lights. Derek the lawyer loped along beside it, shouting at the driver. A woman squad member sat in the back, singing a hymn of faith and defiance through the open window. Her voice sailed out over the crowd noise like a sacred offering, so beautiful.

"Oh, and my purse," said the girl. "I had a little purse."

I shook my head and said, "I'm sorry. We didn't mean this to happen. It's their fault."

"I probably won't get it back, do you think? Probably not," she said. "Shit."

I said, "It's not important. What's important—"

A blast from Lucas's bullhorn cut me off. "Everyone please return to the school bus. Assemble at the school bus." I turned in the direction of his voice. I saw a young man with a hand-held newscam walking slowly backward a couple of feet in front of him, shadowed by someone holding a spotlight with a wide silver reflective rim. The three of them matched their steps, a moving unit.

Lucas looks good, I thought. *He's in control here. Everyone will see we're in control here.*

The girl was not there when I turned back. The crowd had begun to break up by then and was streaming away between the parked cars, making it hard to see for any distance. I touched my left lower eyelash. Grit, not glass.

I scanned the lot, a full 360 degrees; the girl must have run to be so far away. Beside me a man in a black leather jacket was tenderly poking his chest with two fingers, apparently checking for broken ribs. I climbed on a news van's bumper, looked around. The girl had vanished. I headed for the school bus.

Lucas stood by the door, wrapping up a television interview: "Women used to give life. Now they want to take it, too. Personally, I see no reason why they should be allowed to do both." I circled around behind him, careful not to intrude on the picture. I waited until the cameras were gone and Lucas had taken his seat behind the wheel to ask him what we should do about the girl. Did we have a guideline for such cases? Should we drive around and try to find her? Wasn't it our duty as protectors of the weak to inform her of her options?

I watched his knuckles tighten on the steering wheel. "Not feasible," he said, and turned the key. "We've taken enough of a beating here today."

As the school bus pulled out into traffic, I saw the girl with the bleeding ear sitting in a City Transit shelter holding what looked like one of our tracts but might have been a bus schedule. She appeared to be staring straight at me, but my window was jammed and I couldn't call out. I watched her stand up and climb onto a bus whose route number I was unable to read.

On the ride back to church, to lift our spirits, Lucas had us sing "Amazing Grace."

Two

THREE DAYS PASSED, THE GROWTH OF A BILLION CELLS. EYE sockets. Brain stem. Flipperlike limbs. His Kingdom, built to last, is built of flesh. His Will is transmitted through human tissue, a chain of bodies stretching back to Adam's.

We gathered that Sunday night in the basement of the Bryce Street Church of God to screen the tapes of the three local news shows. Lucas stood next to the monitor wielding the remote, pausing and rewinding. Channel 7's coverage troubled him—a case of alarmist editing, he said. Their cameraman, falling, had kept on shooting, catching blurry images of scrambling picketers. These had been intercut with Lucas's interview: words, then chaos, words, then chaos. Outrage spread through the darkened room; I heard hisses and sharp, disgusted snorts. A letter-writing campaign was suggested—pressure applied directly to the sponsors, a tactic that had worked for other groups—but Derek spoke against it. The station might defend itself, he said, by airing the damaging segment again. The motion quickly died.

Lucas, fast-forwarding, summed up the mood: "The media's finished. It's bankrupt. They don't have a single sound argument left, so they resort to artsy bullshit."

Sometimes—not for effect, I believed, but to release the unique frustrations that came with his high position—Lucas cursed.

Channel 2's report was more encouraging. The reporter, a moon-faced Asian girl, stood in a cluster of pro-abortion people, speaking with the odd precision of someone who has overcome an accent. By comparison with hers, the surrounding faces looked grim and distorted, which Lucas said was a comment on their souls. One young man, a shameless camera hog, kept raising a poster above the girl's head: AMERICAN WOMEN, GET UP OFF YOUR BACKS! Chuckles broke out in the back of the room and I heard someone whisper, " 'On their backs' is right. Where the abortion mills put them!"

The best was yet to come, though. The camera pulled back for a wide shot, showing the clinic's front sidewalk flanked by two well-behaved Conscience Squad columns. A handsome black policeman standing off to the edge of the picture turned and mouthed a greeting: "Hi, Mom."

"Exactly," the man beside me said. "*Exactly.*"

Lucas ignored the requests for a replay and said it was time for a coffee break. The Alanon group that had used the room before us had left a full pot of decaf and a tray of cherry Danish. I set a pastry on a paper napkin and thought about going outside. Memories of the disturbance at the clinic were drifting from my brain into my chest, pinching off my air supply.

Someone touched my elbow and I turned.

"Good news," said Mrs. Parshall, one of our senior-citizen members. "My grandniece Melissa is back from San Francisco. She flew in last night, so she wasn't in church, but I'm certain she'll attend next week." She licked a spot of red jelly off her lip; her tongue was thick and gray, like spoiled meat.

"What about the . . . ?" I was going to say "Buddhist sculptor," but that was not right. I couldn't remember what the boyfriend did or what his religion was, only that he did something exotic and worshiped something false.

"Melissa threw him out," said Mrs. Parshall. "She told him to take a hike and he obeyed her."

Knowing Melissa, I doubted this. She was not the type who threw men out. She didn't have the confidence. Melissa was sweet and homely, not all there, and had a well-known history of falling in love with any man who was willing to open a car door for her. There were people in church who called her a whore, but whores get money for what they do, and Melissa asked for nothing but attention. I had never dated her, but I knew men who had. I did not respect those men.

"So, shall I tell her you'll call?" said Mrs. Parshall. "Or drop by the house, why don't you? Either way."

"I'm busy all this week," I said. "I'm sorry. Tell her I'll see her at Bible class on Sunday."

Mrs. Parshall pecked my cheek, moving in so close I had to shut my eyes. Her head had been shaved the year before as part of a cancer operation, and just so we wouldn't forget she'd almost died, she had worn an ugly buzz-cut ever since. Her interest was euthanasia, not abortion—she feared that the next time she went to a hospital she would be put to sleep by overworked, amoral doctors. Our group had a couple of members like her: retired people with no place else to go, nothing on their calendars. I liked to think I sympathized, but the truth was the old folks' helplessness exasperated me.

Impatience was one of my faults—a trait I often repented of but hadn't as yet tried to change. Overcoming lust and drugs was my priority. Minor character flaws would have to wait.

Lucas came up and rested a forearm on Mrs. Parshall's shoulder. "Dorothy, you're a pillar," he said. "Why don't you put on a pot of real coffee? People are losing consciousness here."

Always happy to be of use, Mrs. Parshall did as she was told. Lucas led me into the hallway. The floor was slippery, recently waxed, and smelled of that sickly sweet disinfectant used only in schools and churches.

"The niece has returned," said Lucas. "Our wish come true."

I guessed he was being sarcastic, but with Lucas it was hard to tell. The Navy had trained him not to show fear, which meant he showed little of anything.

"You shouldn't talk like that," I said. "It's hurtful."

Lucas said, "Sometimes I'm hurtful," and pried the childproof cap off a bottle of antidepressant tablets. All of us in the Squad had our faults, and Lucas's Prozac prescription was an open secret. At least he had a good excuse: his wife had divorced him six months ago, convincing the judge that his activism made him an unfit father. His son and daughter, thirteen and eight, had testified against him, repeating elaborate tales of neglect that Lucas said were the product of coaching by hired psychiatrists. Feminist oddballs from out of state had packed the courtroom, supporting the wife. After the trial, she went on a speaking tour—a darling of the other side.

Lucas put three tablets on his tongue (one too many, it seemed to me) and made a bitter face.

"I'm detecting a lack of focus," he said. "The levity in that room disgusted me. Sometimes I wonder who's serious here, or if we're just a bunch of moral dilettantes."

Afraid to speak, I watched his face turn black. Lucas was powerful, physically and spiritually. His moods, when he chose to reveal them, rolled over you like fierce Midwestern weather.

"Reaction?" said Lucas. "Comment? Explanation?"

I suspected that what he wanted from me was an excuse for an outburst, an opening for some speech he'd been rehearsing. The man had been spending too much time alone. Ever since he had lost his wife and children, Lucas had been living out of gym bags, changing motel rooms every few weeks to frustrate attempts at harassment or surveillance. Surveillance was a big issue with Lucas— he claimed to have proof he was under it. Who was watching him he wouldn't say, though one time he showed me a dollar bill and tapped the eye on the pyramid and winked.

"It could be we're just exhausted," I said. I was thinking about the girl at the clinic and feeling bad for how we'd left her there. "Maybe we should cancel next week's meeting."

The twelve-and-under Bible-study class had papered the hall with a series of pictures titled "The Ten Commandments in Action." Lucas glared at the sloppy watercolors. "The group is losing momentum," he said. "Call it the problem of who feeds the dog. Everyone's counting on someone else to do it, and consequently the dog goes unfed. That leaves me to feed it, every night. To think I personally saved half you people, and now, when things get complicated . . ."

I didn't know what he was talking about, but whatever it was, I felt wounded, since I was one of those whom he had baptized. That had been two years ago, when I was twenty-four, at a time in my life when nothing was working and everything I could think of had been tried. Fortunately for me, the Lord is not something you think of.

He appears.

"We have to tighten up," said Lucas. "I want to form a group within the group, a trustworthy inner circle. I'm planning certain activities certain members might not have the stomach for."

"Lucas, you haven't been sleeping," I said. "I'm looking at your cheeks. They're yellow."

He rolled his shoulders, inhaled. "I'm not going to hide it: I *am* tired. Run-down. This business with Deborah . . ." He let out the breath. "Never depend on them, Weaver. Provide for them, love them, but never . . ." He glanced at one of the Ten Commandment posters, the one that showed two stickmen holding knives to each other's throats. "I'm whining now, what garbage. Maybe if you prayed for me . . ."

"I already do," I said. "I pray for everyone."

"Well, concentrate on me," said Lucas. "Weaver, I'm no Hercules. Someone has to help me feed the dog."

Tuesday afternoon the girl called.

I had just got back to my apartment after a long sweaty

day in the car delivering Sanipure sample kits. Sanipure was a Christian corporation based in Kent, Ohio, that purchased soaps and beauty products from leading brand-name manufacturers and put its own cross-shaped labels on them. I had obtained my distributorship through a church friend, Conrad Burns, Sanipure's district supervisor. The job offered flexible hours, which I needed, and "unlimited earning potential"—or so Conrad Burns had always boasted. There were prizes and bonuses based on your performance: appliances, trips to Disney World, cars. But I was not a dedicated salesman and so far I had won nothing. My sales figures rose and fell from week to week depending on my moods and on my church commitments, and there had been months when I hadn't earned a dime. Lately, I'd been on a terrible downswing, partly because I was tired and partly because I'd lost faith in the product. The soaps were overpriced and didn't clean effectively. The makeup made women's skin break out in hives.

I could afford to neglect my sales route because my mother sent me an allowance. She seemed to believe that my taking her money would keep some link between us and eventually lure me back—back from the group, which she did not approve of, and from the whole world of the Bryce Street Church of God. The checks, which she wrote on her business account as if I were some deductible expense, arrived at the end of the month and were always for six hundred dollars. My mother never sent letters with the checks, but sometimes, on the memo line, she scribbled a nagging word or two: "Why are you doing this?" "Let's talk (at home)." Her penmanship was like her voice—hard and slanted, pushy—but I had to admit that her money came in handy. It paid the bills and the rent and allowed me to help the group with odd expenses. In times of special hardship, when the school bus needed repairs or one of us had to post bail for some trumped-up trespassing charge, a hundred dollars could make a real difference. What's more, the thought of my mother's money going to something higher than herself—her option-packed Lincoln Town Car that did everything but cook and serve hot meals, her collection of bad modern African art, her shopping trips to Chicago and New York—was a pleasure in itself.

I slipped off my shoes and set them side by side on an unopened carton of Sanipure detergent. I leafed through the bills on my desk—power, telephone, Visa, an over-due pledge to the Reverend Armand Dale's television ministry—then went to the kitchenette and mixed a glass of Nestlé's Quik, drinking half and leaving half for later. I switched on a motivational cassette tape I'd been lis-tening to for the past few days—*The Path to Mental Mastery*—and picked up a single twenty-pound dumb-bell. I had broken my arm in a car wreck last winter (my fault, I was drunk on vodka, a stupid weekend lapse), and though the cast had come off months ago, the muscles of my left side still overpowered the muscles of my right. I was into my fifth set of concentration curls, lifting for definition, when the phone rang.

"Is this the Walquist residence?"

I grunted and tried to catch my breath.

"I was wondering, just an idea, if maybe you'd like to go dancing tonight. Maybe you people don't dance, though. Do you? We could maybe have that talk you mentioned."

I recognized the voice. I sensed that the girl was nearby, around the corner, and I wondered how she'd tracked me down. The traffic noises coming through the phone line seemed to match the ones outside my window.

"I want you to tell me your name," I said, adopting an authoritative tone. I reached for a pad and pencil and jotted down the date: *July 11.* "Unless we have certain information, we won't be able to—"

"Kim," she said.

"Kim what?"

A mucousy smoker's cough, then silence.

I crossed to the window, looked down. A U-Haul being unloaded at the curb was blocking my view of the corner phone booth.

"Kim, we really do care for you," I said. *Refuses to state last name.* "Please don't feel judged or intimidated—our only concern is your health."

"You mean, am I still knocked up?" she said. "Yeah, I guess I am."

"That is such excellent news, Kim." *Unborn child fine.* "I know you're confused now, but choosing life is always, always worth it. When was the baby conceived?"

"At night."

I sighed to show disappointment in her attitude. "A month ago? Two months? This isn't a joke, Kim. Not to me and not, I hope, to you."

"I don't know. Six weeks ago. Maybe closer to seven."

I heard sniffling. Either Kim had a cold or she was crying. Fragile, in any case. Possibly drugged. I wondered if I should ask her straight out: "Are you taking something?" and let her know I understood because I had been there myself. She might be offended, though, and I could lose her. One more young woman sedated on a table, sacrificing everything to a surgeon's pointed instruments.

"Oh, you know what?" she said, sounding brighter. "I

found my stupid purse. Nobody'd even bothered to open it. That's when I knew how crazy that scene was: money on the ground and no one cared."

The line went crackly then, a surge of static. Kim spoke over it: "Maybe you can answer this: If you have a career but not much money, and you have a baby, does the government have to . . . ?"

I wasn't up to this; I lacked the training. "I want you to call someone, Kim—a lawyer friend named Derek Griff. I want you to write down his number."

Kim said, "He's the guy who gave me yours. I saw his name in the *Pioneer Press*. I told him I needed to reach the human roadblock." She blew the phone line full of cigarette smoke, and I wondered if she had any idea that her unborn child was being poisoned. "If you're not in the mood to go out tonight," she said, "I won't be crushed for life or anything."

"Do you really think dancing's appropriate?" I said. "In your present situation?"

Kim said, "What's my present situation?"

"That is what we are trying to determine. Maybe if you phoned my lawyer friend—"

I heard a click, and I thought she'd hung up. Then she said: "I can't believe I called. If you really wanted to help me out so badly, you would have come home on the bus with me that day. I know you saw me sitting there."

"I did," I said. "I'm sorry. Things were out of control. . . ."

"No kidding."

"It wasn't our fault," I said. "We didn't want that. Unfortunately, the media twists things, and—"

"Oh, I see," Kim said. "You're one of those."

"Those what?"

Then she really did hang up.

I hustled downstairs in my stocking feet and jogged up the street to the phone booth. On the shelf beside the phone, I found a pass to a nightclub, torn in half, and a balled-up, lipsticky Kleenex. I called out Kim's name as I circled the block. I could feel pieces of glass and sidewalk grit nicking the soles of my feet, but I kept going. I walked for half an hour, trying to ignore the pain and thinking that if I absorbed enough of it God would help me find her.

It was crucial.

At seven weeks the fetus forms eyelids.

At eleven, hands.

Three

WHEN YOU CAN SEE THINGS OTHERS CAN'T—CHILDREN IN THE womb, the hand of God—they call you a fanatic. But you know better what you are: a person with vision. They hate your vision. They want you to squint at the world the way they do and miss what they miss: real evil, real good.

I was not raised religious. My mother owned a successful liquor store in Cedar Lake, Wisconsin, a town of seven thousand people just a mile from the Minnesota border. Because Wisconsin's blue laws were laxer than Minnesota's (the drinking age was eighteen, not twenty-one, and stores could stay open late and on Sundays), my mother could charge what she pleased for her liquor and still do twice the volume of the nearest Minnesota stores.

That fact, and my father's life insurance policy—he died when I was two, in a drunken Montana elk-hunting mishap—made my mother a wealthy woman. She owned the largest house in town, the largest car. Her beds were always kings. Size was important to her, sheer size. And it wasn't because she had grown up poor, because she hadn't. Her father was a lawyer. No, the reason she loved large things, I think, was that she was tall for a woman, six foot one, and lying on a king-size mattress, watching a big-screen color TV while reading a novel six inches thick, made her feel petite.

Me, I felt tiny, less than petite, but I was just a child. Maybe all children feel as small as I did, as if they might just fall in and disappear while sitting on a parent's lap. I don't have any brothers or sisters, so I wouldn't know.

Of the church buildings in Cedar Lake, only St. Mark's Presbyterian even approached the size of our house. As far as I remember, we never set foot in any of them, and their smallness was part of the reason ("Why should we sit in some crowded church," my mother used to say, "when we have all this wonderful space to ourselves?"). Religion to her was a joke, a farce, although she said she was glad it existed. After all, it was pious Minnesota— "Lutheranland," she called it—that made her liquor business what it was. Once, when I was twelve or thirteen, I picked up the upstairs telephone and heard my mother tell her father that her greatest fear in life was that the Minnesota Lutherans would relax their morals and let their eighteen-year-olds drink.

But pastors and priests were all hypocrites, according to my mother. They sinned as much as other people. More. One of her steadiest customers, she used to love to tell me, was the local Methodist minister, who bought Canadian whiskey by the case and had it delivered after dark to a small lakeside cabin north of town where he went to write his sermons. My mother claimed that inside the cabin there was a four-foot stack of *Playboys* and a projector for showing dirty movies. I remember asking her how she knew all this. "I brought him his order one night," she said. "The bastard said he'd have my store closed down if I spread what I saw. A man of God."

I believed my mother's story; she was not a liar. And though she did not respect religion, she was strict with herself and free of vices. I never saw her drink or smoke or gamble. Her boyfriends, as a rule, were not allowed inside our house, and if she ever slept with them, it could only have been on her trips out of town. As a woman in the liquor trade, she said, she simply couldn't afford to slip up—the community was watching her, watching her social life, watching me. But far from resenting this pressure, my mother seemed to treat it as a challenge. On Sundays, when the cars streamed past our house on their way to services, my mother would wake me up early and lead me into the yard to wash her car, mow the lawn, rake leaves, and put on a show of mother-son togetherness that lasted until the cars had all gone back.

One Sunday our project was standing on a ladder and filling the space above our front door with tall stick-on letters: THE WALQUISTS'. What made me sad about the sign was that there were only two of us Walquists.

My mother had nothing to hide or be ashamed of, but that was her sin. The Sin of Pride. She had all the answers, knew all the tricks. She started half of her sentences with "Speaking as a businesswoman" and ended them with "at least in my opinion." And she didn't just speak to adults that way, but to my friends and me.

We would ask her if we could go swimming in the gravel pit or camp overnight in the woods behind the house, and that's how my mother would answer: by giving her opinion as a businesswoman.

By the time I entered junior high, I was sick of my mother the businesswoman. All we did was fight. A lot of our fights were about TV: she wanted me to watch more of it. She said TV would broaden my horizons, would lift me above our small-town life and put me in touch with the world at large. But I did not want my horizons broadened. I knew that the broader they got, the smaller I would feel, and I felt small enough already. No, what I really wanted—and what my mother the businesswoman never understood, reclining in her mammoth rocker, paging through one of her five-pound novels with manicured fingers the size of pinking shears—was to be big right there in Cedar Lake.

I smoked my first pot in seventh grade, at a friend's house out by the county landfill, where I was not supposed to go because I might step on a nail and get tetanus and ruin a day in the busy life my mother plotted out each January in her *New Yorker* appointment calendar.

My friend's uncle rolled the joints. He showed us how to do shotguns. He would put the lit end of a joint in his mouth, seal his lips around it, and bring his face so close to mine that I could see dirt on the hairs inside his nostrils. The smoke jetted into my lungs as he blew. At first, nothing happened. A charcoal taste, some coughing. Then, a moment later, a huge transparent bubble formed around me. The bubble was filmy and tough; it clung to me like the plastic wrap on a supermarket beef roast. My words when I spoke—"I'm high. Am I high now?"—could not break through the bubble's walls, but stuck there, an inch from my mouth, dammed up, while my friend and his uncle peered in at me, grinning. There was a can of Pepsi on the table, but I was sure that if I tried to drink it, the pop would spill down the front of the bubble and stain the green shag carpet at my feet.

My friend's uncle asked me what was wrong. When I couldn't answer him, he inflated my lungs with another shotgun.

Having feelings you can't describe, and having them often, makes you lonely. Getting stoned made me lonely, but getting more stoned made it seem all right. The bubble was always there, a perfect, soundproof seal, but depending on how much pot I smoked I could make it grow large enough to include other people and outside objects. Then I could talk to my friends and be heard. I could drink things and not have them run down my shirt.

What I liked to drink most was vodka, because it has no taste and doesn't stain. I stole the bottles from my mother's stockroom, where I sometimes worked on summer weekends. At first I put the losses down to breakage, but later on, a deliveryman for one of the liquor distributors showed me how we could fill out an invoice so he would get his money and I would get free vodka. Halfway through my sophomore year in high school, I was trading the stolen liquor for pot, and when there wasn't pot in town, for pills. Some of these pills came straight from Dr. Harkham, an osteopath who sometimes did work on my mother's always-aching back. His office was in the back of his house, a few doors down from ours, and was filled with elaborate osteopathic equipment made of polished chrome. Though Dr. Harkham was married, he liked to sit me down on his complicated tables and ask about my girlfriends—what I did with them, how their bodies felt. Once, he put his arm around me and asked who I thought was more handsome, Burt Reynolds or Robert Redford.

The more time I spent with people like the doctor, the more I learned about my town: that underneath it there were secret passageways with doors that opened on strange, illicit places. Basement rec rooms with slot machines that took real quarters and seldom gave them back. An old stone barn with a swept dirt floor where farmers sat on folding chairs, betting on grisly dogfights. A trailer-home meth lab equipped with tubes and beakers where I once saw a man catch his shirtsleeve on fire by brushing it against a Bunsen burner—but instead of putting the sleeve out in the sink, he waved it flaming through the air and screamed that he was a demon from Hell and fire couldn't harm him. I got to know all of these places and where the guns that protected them were kept. I met older women who liked to do things, liked to have things done to them. Soon, I felt safer inside these secret places than I did at home, paralyzed behind THE WALQUISTS' sign.

I would sit on my bed with headphones on, getting into heavy metal, and exhale marijuana smoke through the window fan. To hide my pot breath, I gargled with Listerine, then spit it out in the mayonnaise jar hidden under my bed. When the coast was clear, I would dump out the jar in the flower garden beneath my bedroom window. On weekends, my mother the businesswoman worked in that garden, weeding and spraying, coaxing along the enormous hybrid roses she exhibited at the county fair each August. Once, I dreamed she unearthed a human jawbone and set it on my pillow with a note: "Where are the other victims buried?"

My friends and I sneaked out at night with cans of black spray paint and wrote on barns and bridges: *Satan Rules! The Beast Be With Us! 666. Destruktion!* We copied the words out of horror comic books and off the backs of record albums bought from a store in St. Paul called Hidden Planet. The storeowner's name was Malcolm Moon. He sold us incense, tarot cards, and books on black magic. He pierced my right ear. The cheap steel stud he first inserted there soon crusted over with yellowy pus and was replaced by a silver Grateful Dead skull.

The next thing I knew, my grades had dropped and I was quitting the high-school football team, which I had only joined in the first place as an excuse to wear a helmet and add a few inches to my average height. My personal hygiene deteriorated. One night I woke up in bed, my crotch on fire, and saw black bugs go scurrying down the sheets. The woman I knew I had caught them from took me into the shower in her trailer and scrubbed my whole body with tingly Rid-X, then pulled me down onto her water bed and infested me again. A few days later my mother the businesswoman found an insect on the toilet seat.

She captured it on a piece of Scotch tape and held it in front of my nose. "What is this?"

"A lice."

"Correction: a *louse*," she said. "It's singular."

"I bet if you look, you'll find more," I said.

"Do I dare ask where it came from?"

"My cock."

My mother raised her hand to slap me. She couldn't do it, though, which cracked me up. I asked her if, as a businesswoman, as a respected businesswoman, she found me disgusting—in her opinion.

"My son is trying to make me cry," she said. "I don't know why he's doing that. Does he?"

I stood there. Then she said, "Of course he doesn't. His father didn't know either."

"Leave him out of it."

"He killed himself, you know," she said, twisting the beads on her garish turquoise choker. "Maybe it wasn't intentional, but it was suicide all the same. The man was just fatally stupid."

"You cunt."

"He used to call me that, too," my mother said. "Usually, it meant I'd won a point."

The day of my high-school graduation, after a year of not talking to each other except to excuse ourselves from the table or pass on important telephone messages, my mother the businesswoman gave me a calfskin Pierre Cardin wallet stuffed with twenty-dollar bills. "I want you to leave now," she said, "and take the Chrysler. I don't care where you go—just go. You're jeopardizing my reputation here."

I moved to St. Paul and got a job helping Malcolm Moon at Hidden Planet. I learned to mix the essences and powders that went into "Andronicus" and "Venus," his herbal aphrodisiacs. I got to know the customers. There was a boy named Tim, a runaway, sixteen years old, with a running herpes sore under his sparse blond mustache. Tim would buy vitamin E pills at the store, bite them open in front of me, and rub the oil on his lip. There was a woman named Constance Ann, beautiful, in her forties, who told me she threw the I Ching for a living. She also claimed to be writing a book that proved Robert Kennedy shot JFK because he blamed him for Marilyn's death. I liked these people, but I could not talk to them—we were all too stoned—and eventually Malcolm Moon let me go. After that I worked at a McDonald's, on the management track because I'd finished high school. But I washed out of that job, too. I just wasn't comfortable giving orders to black women twice my age.

And all the while, the bubble was behind me, two steps back and gaining. Sometimes, driving alone in my car, even when I wasn't loaded, I would feel a sudden jump of pressure deep inside my ears. The car would float up off the road a few feet, and I would go skimming through space, no traction, as if it were all a computer game and I were not in the car at all, but back in my mother's big house, in my bedroom, operating a joystick.

Then, the August I turned twenty-five, my life hit bottom and I almost died. A born-again Christian named Lucas Boone found me passed out on the men's-room floor of the St. Paul Greyhound station, choking on vomit and Darvocet pain pills. I hadn't intended to die, exactly, just to sedate myself before a bus trip. I had a ticket for New Mexico, where I planned to camp out alone in the desert, permanently stoned, and be the tallest thing for miles around. Lucas loaded me into his car, rushed me to a hospital, then waited for over an hour while the doctors pumped my stomach under a brilliant fluorescent light bulb that burned on my retinas for hours afterward. And that's when my second, my real life began—my life in Jesus Christ.

I studied and fasted for six weeks straight, reading the Holy Bible twice through and praying ceaselessly for inner healing. I tossed out my earrings, my drug stash, and all my tapes and records. I arose from the waters of baptism clean, a whole new human, dripping wet, and dried myself off with a scratchy white towel. I looked around at all the smiling people holding out their arms to me, and all of them—this was the miracle—were my size and seemed to be able to hear me when I spoke.

Four

I ASKED THE NURSE AT THE CLINIC'S FRONT DESK TO LET ME see last week's appointment schedule. She answered that such information was privileged. I said I knew that but this was an emergency. She narrowed her already narrow eyes and told me to go fuck myself.

"Good old auto-intercourse," I said. "You have a truly delightful mind."

"Don't you people have *lives*?" the nurse said. "Really, I mean it. Don't you ever *work*?"

I opened up with a stream of nonsense syllables: "Sobaba, sobaba, sobabaso . . . ," then said, "No, we're too busy speaking in tongues."

The nurse touched a glowing red button on her phone.

"Security, I have a man out here. One of our Christian-soldier, Nazi-youth friends."

I said, "Who is that? The janitor? I happen to know you don't employ a guard here."

"As of last week we do," the nurse said. "Name of Hector. Six foot five. Tattoos. Aims for the testicles, instant vasectomy."

"Delightful," I said.

On my way out I slipped a few tracts into the magazine rack—bloody ones.

At the bus shelter where I had last seen Kim, I ate fried chicken out of a bag and studied the posted maps and schedules. The stop served three different routes; they originated downtown, only a few blocks away, and ended in the western suburbs. I ruled out one route immediately, the twelve, which ran express to the airport and on to the multipurpose domed stadium. The ten was a local, residential route, but the neighborhoods it passed through—Oxford Hill, Old Laurel, Rexington—seemed too established and wealthy for Kim or, for that matter, anyone who commuted by bus. That left the nine, whose path across town formed a kind of contour map of blight. According to the logic of the nine, the shortest route between two bad neighborhoods was a long curving detour around the nearest good one.

Kim, I was sure of it, lived along the nine.

The man I sat down next to in the shelter eyed my grease-stained bag of chicken bones. He was one of those semi-well-dressed bums you see in public libraries hunched over stacks of Time-Life picture books, pretending to do intense vital research while furtively kneading their genitals. He seemed to be having trouble asking for my lunch bag, but judging by the handkerchief tucked in the pocket of his thrift-shop suit coat, I knew he would be polite when he did. I waited for him to speak up and thought about just giving him the bag. What was more humiliating, I wondered: having to beg for someone's cold chicken bones or being offered them?

He drew himself up to full height, a good six feet, and cleared his throat dramatically. "How soon human beings forget," he said, "what a privilege it is to live in freedom. A privilege, not an honor. An honor would mean we deserved it. We do not. Both Lincoln and Shakespeare are clear on that point."

Slowly, nobly, he turned and faced me. His coat reeked of mothballs. His lips were hugely cracked. "Public transport," he said. "I use it, I do not abuse it."

It was noon, and hot, and the chicken smell was so strong I felt guilty, as if I were purposely teasing the man. I watched his tongue lick around inside his cheek.

"I use public transport," he said, "for convenience. Not because I deserve to. I do not. My letters of thanks are on file with the state, a matter of public record."

The nine bus was only a stoplight away; I decided to take the direct approach. I opened my wallet and stripped out a bill. "Let me buy you lunch, sir. Courtesy of the Bryce Street Church of God."

The man cleared his throat, reared back, and let go a stringy, high-arcing gob that made a dark line on the sidewalk when it dropped. "A sandwich," he said. "I'd like a deli sandwich. I know a place nearby with famous tongue." He spat again, uncontrollably, it seemed—a shocking foamy load that barely cleared his knees.

I put down the bill on the bench, seeing too late that it

was a twenty, and weighted it with the bag of bones. Then I stood up to get on the bus.

"Son, you've forgotten something."

I turned.

The man leaned forward and handed me the bill.

"If you're not going to join me," he said, "I don't want this. Spend it on yourself."

He fished out a drumstick from the bag of bones and began to gnaw.

The driver was a middle-aged black man with runny red eyes that patrolled the rearview mirror, checking on some delinquents in the back. He drove the bus as if it were on rails, speeding up and changing lanes without appearing to look at the road. His sweat-stained shirt was open to the breastbone, and I could see a fat gold crucifix reflected in the windshield. I didn't approve of sacred jewelry—rock musicians and fashion models had robbed it of meaning, I felt—but on the driver the cross looked functional, worn for protection, not display.

The kids in back grew quieter as the bus climbed a hill and left the business district, turning onto a street of low brick houses. The small weedy yards were lands of enchantment, where bearded dwarves and knock-kneed fawns stood among towering plastic daisies whose fan-blade petals revolved in the breeze. In one yard a plaster Nativity scene, apparently a year-round decoration, was under siege by huge ceramic frogs. Next door, a bonneted Mother Goose led her goslings past a French château. I did not see any people in the yards and not a single dog or cat. No one got on or off the bus and the driver cruised past the stops at full speed.

"I'm hoping that you can help me," I said, catching the driver's attention in the rearview. "I'm looking for a girl who rides this bus. At least I know she rode it last Thursday."

The driver hushed me, finger to his lips. "Not while the bus is in motion," he said. "Too many transit inspectors around."

I looked around at the other passengers. If anyone was an inspector, it was me. Everyone else was too young, too old, or too drunk.

"Of course if you were one," the driver said, "I would have been busted already. For these." He raised his right hand and wiggled the fingers, showing off his rings. "To me, miraculous healing crystals of amethyst and sapphire. To them, a violation of the dress code."

I leaned in closer. "Maybe you remember her. She got on downtown at the clinic stop last Thursday morning."

The driver nodded. "Lots of commotion. Lots of cops that day."

"The girl's in her early twenties," I said.

The driver waved at an oncoming bus and got an identical wave in return from the white-haired lady at its wheel. "Give me a face," he said. "I need a face. Pregnant girl is not enough description."

I was startled. I said, "That's right. She's pregnant."

The driver shifted down and braked. "I know my route," he said. "Lots of girls who use that stop are pregnant. At least when they get off they are. When they get back on, I don't ask questions." He opened the door for an Oriental man, letting the man's three children on for free. "Tell me again what she looks like," he said.

I tried to project Kim's face on the window. At first all I saw was an oval blank. Straight blond hair appeared, but framing nothing. I realized I'd been afraid to look too closely, afraid she didn't want me to. I concentrated harder, on her body, but it had been almost two years since I had dated, and I no longer noticed women's figures. I recalled that Kim's hand when I held it felt thin, so perhaps she was thin all over. Also, I was sure her eyes were blue, but so were the eyes of most Midwestern girls. Typically Midwestern—that was the best I could do. But very thin. A malnourished cheerleader type.

And then it came to me. "Her ear was bleeding. She had a bloody ear."

The driver sat up straighter and eyed me in the rearview. "What's her name?"

"I thought I already told you: Kim."

"Matter of fact, you did not," the driver said. "You must be her man, though. She said you'd come looking, and here you are, zipper-cased Bible and all."

"You're kidding."

"I told you I know my route," he said, "and that's what a route is: passengers. I had to make sure it was you, though, not some pervert. It sounds to me like you hardly know the girl."

"We only just met," I said.

The driver winked at me via the rearview. "I guess what's important," he said, "is she knows you. May all men be so blessed." There was a flash of purple crystal as he pointed a finger at the windshield. "Her stop's that next one coming up. Brick apartment building on the corner."

I stood with my Bible tucked under my arm, thanked the driver for all his help, then rushed down the steps as the double doors parted, eager to get busy saving lives.

Five

IN THE BUILDING'S CONCRETE COURTYARD, BAREFOOT CHILDREN with sunburned ears peered at me over the handlebars of their plastic Big Wheel tricycles. The low-riding brats appeared poised to charge, their splayed-out knees raised high, their grimy prehistoric-looking toes curled around the pedals. I asked the one who seemed to be the leader if he knew a girl named Kim. He plugged a thumb in his mouth and shook his head. Garbled voices from hidden TV sets drifted down through the open windows, voices of actors and game-show announcers, phonies on the coasts.

I looked in all four entryways, but the names on the mailboxes there were last names. I walked back out to the courtyard. The kids and their Big Wheels had vanished. I stood there for a moment, fingering my Scriptures and looking down at a pair of handprints someone had made in the concrete back when it was wet. Was the person alive or dead, I wondered, and had he done anything else to be remembered by, or were the handprints all? It was the sort of tricky, moody question that used to come to me inside the bubble and make me think I would always be alone. I had to guard against that now. Be positive. According to *The Path to Mental Mastery*, thoughts are actual objects in the mind on their way to becoming objects in the world. I squared my shoulders and called out, "Kim—hello! Kim, it's Weaver Walquist!"

No one answered.

I called again, with more authority.

Off to my right a man yelled, "Keep it down," and I heard a window slam shut. Then, above me, another window opened. A woman's voice said, "What do you know. I just won a ten-dollar bet with myself."

I looked up at Kim, who was leaning out over me, her hands braced on the windowsill. A purple towel was wrapped around her head and a white towel around her chest. The white one was wrapped more loosely, and this time I couldn't help noticing her figure. It was very nice, I thought: much healthier looking than I remembered. From everything I could make out, Kim was the classic quarterback's girlfriend—just the type who buys the modern lie that there is more to life, more fun and more excitement, than merely passing life on.

"If it isn't a good time to talk . . . ," I said.

"Don't be dumb. I'm almost dressed," she said. "Come up, it's apartment Four-B."

She unwound the towel from her head, bent forward, and squeezed out her long wet hair with both hands, then gave it a shake and a toss.

It sprinkled me.

Kim's apartment was small and overdecorated. The convertible sofa was heaped with floral throw pillows. A jungle of potted ferns and spider plants hung from chains screwed into the ceiling, reminding me of the ape room at the zoo. On the patched plaster walls, in silvery frames, there were posters from New York art exhibitions (impressionist lilies, ballerinas, standard dorm-room stuff), a couple of blown-up *Far Side* cartoons, and a pinup shot of a muscle-bound male model straddling a Harley-Davidson and tipping back a long-neck Miller High Life. Dishes of rose-petal potpourri gave the air an intense dusty sweetness, and everywhere I saw tilting stacks of magazines: *Vogue, Cosmopolitan, Vanity Fair.* I noticed a row of family photo-portraits—the kind you have taken at Sears or Woolworth's, with backgrounds of sky and fakey pink clouds—lined up on top of the television set. In the group shot I counted five people: a man and a woman, both smiling, and three poker-faced children, none of whom looked comfortable in their stiff polyester formalwear. Kim had a bandaged hand in the picture and must have been about twelve years old. In all, it looked like just the sort of family Americans dream of having: dumb and loving.

I heard a toilet flush, and Kim said, "Out in a second. Sit down anywhere."

I blushed and didn't move. I looked around for signs of a boyfriend—sweat socks, hand tools, car magazines —but didn't find any. This was a girl's place. The man in Kim's life, who I hoped was the father, had left no trace of himself that I could see. It was hard to imagine he'd ever been in here, or that any man had, before me.

Kim came out of the bathroom wearing a pink sleeveless T-shirt knotted at the midriff and white denim shorts, the kind that come from the store already cut off and frayed. She said she'd been dressing, but it looked to me as though she'd been undressing. I caught myself cutting my eyes at her belly—pale, a little doughy, but not a pregnant belly. Not too pregnant.

"You found me," she said. "That's terrific. Now we can have our important talks, and so on."

"Whatever you want. It's up to you," I said, trying to sound relaxed and flexible. I couldn't afford to scare Kim off again. I adopted the casual, hands-in-pockets stance of the Sanipure salesman who simply wants a hearing.

"Maybe we need some Kool-Aid," Kim said. "Tropical berry or lime?"

"Whichever," I said. Kim stood there. "Tropical berry," I said. The wild choice.

Kim crossed the room to the kitchenette and squatted in front of a compact fridge whose door was covered with famous-painting postcards held on by heart-shaped magnets. The ragged end of her sun-bleached ponytail tickled her thin, freckled shoulders as she took an ice tray from the freezer. I could see the crack of her butt above her cutoffs, a dainty dark notch that was trouble to look at.

As Kim poured the punch into two tall glasses, I set down my Bible on the breakfast bar. The Bible's vinyl case was slick with sweat. I wiped it dry with a paper towel when Kim turned her back to whack the ice tray against a counter edge.

"I'm sorry about when you phoned last night," I said.

"I sounded pretty rigid. Actually, I'm not a rigid person."

Kim said, "Neither am I, so don't sweat it." She dropped a big ice cube into my glass, and I watched it spin down to the bottom as it melted. "This is my favorite flavor," she said. "They just introduced it this year. You like it?"

I swallowed and raised my eyebrows, licked my lips, aware that I was overdoing something.

"I sort of admire them for it," said Kim.

"Admire who?"

"The Kool-Aid people." She took a lip-staining sip of dark red punch. "Their product's a joke, but they don't seem to know it. They keep on trying new flavors, different sweeteners. It's like they're really convinced that Kool-Aid's good for you. That it's not just empty American death food, like Twinkies or Raviolios. Remember Raviolios?"

"I wasn't allowed to eat them," I said. "My mother said they had rodent hairs in them."

"Exactly," said Kim. "Like hot dogs."

I nodded.

"Well, in my house that's *all* we ate," said Kim. "All those foods they say have rodent hairs. Now, it's kind of kitsch to eat that stuff, but in those days it felt like welfare city. Have some more tropical berry?"

Though I wasn't thirsty, I said, "Sure."

Kim refilled my glass. "Maybe we need some music," she said. "I have a fairly decent stereo. Lifelike sound is my one big indulgence. Otherwise, I'm your standard starving artist."

"Whatever you want to hear," I said.

I saw Kim glance at a shelf of cassette tapes and do a

quick mental inventory. "I mostly listen to rap and thrash these days, but maybe you'd like something soft. Some gospel, maybe?"

"Just because I'm a Christian," I said, holding up an index finger, "doesn't mean I don't like rap and thrash." I was speaking for the record, and not entirely honestly. And then, because this had been bothering me: "Please don't take this wrong, but why do you say 'maybe' all the time? You say it a lot."

Kim looked at me and frowned. "You noticed that."

I shrugged.

Kim said, "I'll have to think that one over. It's something I only do around men. Ashamed of my intelligence, I guess. Little Miss Airhead America. Fly me."

She went to the coffee table by the sofa and returned with a cigarette clamped tough-guy style in the corner of her mouth. She tossed back her hair and held it to her neck and bent down over the gas stove to light the cigarette, then took a seat at the breakfast bar across from me. "I decided the music can wait," she said. "It's not appropriate." She tapped off her ash in an empty punch glass and looked me in the eye, using the challenging, sizing-up expression I recognized from my Sanipure route as a sure sign of an easy mark. "Because now that we've talked about rat hairs and my *maybe*'s, dispensed with the introductions," Kim said, "I'd like you to tell me exactly who you are."

A Christian should welcome the chance to tell his story. His story is the light he must not hide. It should be told with feeling, fully, not to make him look good or to make nonbelievers look bad, but to convey a higher message.

Those were the rules I followed with Kim. I told her about the drugs, but also about my baptism. I told her about my mother the businesswoman, but also about the pastor of my church and his wonderful work with disadvantaged teens. The point was balance, perspective, and when I felt I had said all that mattered, I gave a brief witness for Christ and said, "It's your turn."

Her full name was Kimberly Agnes Lindgren. The details of her life emerged slowly, revealed to me one at a time over a couple of hours, as if she feared that I'd lose interest in her as soon as I knew everything. Mostly, she stuck to the facts. She was twenty-three years old. She had studied design at Lakewood Junior College but had gone broke and dropped out in her third semester. Her parents lived on a dairy farm in eastern North Dakota, where she and her brother and sister had been raised. Up until two weeks ago, when she found out she was pregnant and stopped getting out of bed in the morning, she had worked in a Kinko's copy shop near the university. She told me she hadn't enjoyed the job but had done it to support the work she loved: writing what she called "weird poems and sayings" and trying to sell them to greeting-card companies. She said she had written hundreds of these and designed the illustrations to go with them, but had sold only four or five. I asked to see them.

"I don't know," she said. "I need to get my nerve up. Maybe I'll do these dishes first."

She took away our empty bowls of macaroni and cheese and scraped them out in the sink, then ran the tap. She squirted in some liquid soap with an elbowy throwing motion. I was spellbound. It had been years since a girl had cooked me dinner, and the simple things women do in the kitchen struck me after so much time as almost too fresh and vivid to bear.

After she finished drying the dishes, Kim went into the other room—her "studio," she called it—and reappeared holding a large black portfolio.

"I only show off the one card," she said. "The other ones aren't any good." She sat down on the sofa next to me and laid the portfolio on the coffee table, squaring the corners with the table edge.

"First," she said, lighting a menthol 100, "a little explanation. The greeting-card industry's changing. Fast. It's not just Hallmark anymore. Ducklings and balloons and kittens—all that silly shit they did, all that sentimental stuff—is out. What's in is sick humor. And that means opportunity."

"How so?"

"Because it's bad for Hallmark. The new stuff is too surreal for them, too twisted. They try to keep up, but they can't, they're just too stuffy. Their idea of a trendy Christmas card is making Santa—oh, I don't know— black. And instead of saying 'Ho, ho, ho,' maybe he says, 'Yo, yo, yo.' See what I mean? It's banal."

I looked at Kim's face, which was red with excitement. That vein I sometimes noticed on men's temples, but never on women's, was pulsing fiercely. I wondered how often she got in this state and what effect it might have on the baby. Combined with the smoking, it couldn't be good.

"Anyway," she said, slowing down a bit, "there's plenty of room now for free-lancers like me. Because there are all these new companies, see, and they can be really adventurous." Hesitantly, with care, she opened the portfolio. "I warn you," she said, "it's kind of different."

Kim slid the card from beneath its plastic cover-sheet and stood it on edge on the table. On the front of the card a diapered man, his arms and legs in casts, lay on his back in a hospital bed, attached to a network of levers, ropes, and pulleys. Cartoon nurses in miniskirts and heels stood around the bed, operating the traction device. The caption on the top was, *Wishing you the very best of care.*

"But then," said Kim, "you open it up and—"

I didn't expect to be shocked, but I was. By pulling on the ropes, presumably, the nurses had turned the man over on his stomach and lifted him off the bed. Spread-eagled under him was a naked nurse. Wavy lines around the patient's buttocks (his diapers lay on the floor now) indicated vigorous motion. The patient's butt and the nurse's breasts were made of a fuzzy felt material that struck me as more obscene than the picture.

I said, "You're right, it's different. It's also pretty hilarious."

Kim sat back and crossed her arms and eyed me. "Why don't you say what you *really* think?"

"I did. It's a witty get-well card."

Kim said, "Maybe you didn't hear me clearly. This isn't some little hobby for me—this is my *career.*"

After I told Kim I realized that, after I looked her square in the eye and told her I was sorry, I asked to see another card.

Kim looked away from me, down at her portfolio. Her temple pulsed twice as hard as before. "You lied about the nurses card, you'll lie about the rest," she said.

"That's not fair. I didn't lie."

"When you say something's funny but don't even laugh, that's a lie, in my book."

I stared at the rug for a moment, absorbing the justice

of that. Brittle, brown spider-plant debris was every-where.

Eventually, Kim said, "Fine. Who cares. My other fa-vorite card's a birthday card. It shows a baby and a cake with candles. Grown-ups are standing around in party hats." She drew her legs up onto the couch and tucked them under her, straining the half-open zipper of her cut-offs. "Over the cake it says, 'Baby, don't blow it! You'll never be thirty-nine again.' The 'blow it' refers to the candles. It's inane."

I shook my head and said, "I disagree. In my opinion, it's better than the nurses one. I like the subtlety."

Kim hugged a throw pillow close to her chest, pushing the tops of her breasts into view. "Maybe you should go now. I think we'd better talk some other time."

"Now you're being insecure."

"Fine, I admit it," she said. "I'm also tired. I get in-credibly tired nowadays."

"That's normal," I said. "The tiredness is normal."

Kim put the greeting cards back in her portfolio. "Now, you're *really* bugging me. Please leave. Maybe we'll talk this weekend or something, when we're both in better moods."

I nodded and spread my hands on my knees, preparing to stand up.

"By the way," Kim said, "about adoption."

I turned my head and didn't stand.

"Adoption is not a choice for me," said Kim. "I'm to-tally against it. My best friend in school was adopted—practically my only friend—and she committed suicide the day she turned eighteen. She used to tell me she'd never felt loved and that she didn't think she ever would. I just thought you should know that."

There wasn't much I could say. I asked some questions about the friend, but Kim did not want to talk about her, saying the girl was dead and that was that. I told her I thought she was being extreme, not to mention illogical, by basing her view of adoption on a tragic isolated case. Kim said, "So I'm illogical. Sue me. *Everything's* an isolated case."

A few minutes later, I let myself out, but I left my Bible there—on the breakfast bar next to the toaster. I knew that even if Kim didn't read it, she would have to look at it or touch it in order to put it away. I also knew that, sometimes, when a person is truly lost in this world, suffocating inside her private bubble where all she can hear is her own droning heartbeat, a touch can be enough.

Six

SERVICES THAT SUNDAY BEGAN AN HOUR EARLY BECAUSE REVerend Spannring had a flight to catch. He was flying to Salt Lake City for a conference on child pornography. A national group had agreed to pay his way, so we had no objections to the trip. We had to be careful spending church funds on things that were not emergencies. Over the last few months, offerings had been tailing off along with the general economy, and the chapel, which had been built by volunteers from odd-sized donated cinder blocks, was starting to fall apart. The plastic stained-glass windows were warping in their frames. The roof leaked. Now and then, on rainy days, dirty puddles would form in the aisles on the indoor-outdoor carpeting.

I stood in the lobby greeting people as they came in

from the parking lot. The regulars seemed grumpy and were slow to arrive. The now-and-thens did not show up at all. Sundays at the Bryce Street Church of God had always been unpredictable; our faith was a flickering flame. At times, it burned like a bonfire and roared through the chapel and reddened people's faces. It flung us around in our seats, making our eyes water, searing our lungs, causing us to shout and gasp and weep. At other times, the fire was low and steady, set at simmer, good for meditation. Once in a while, it went out entirely.

Conrad Burns came in with his wife and immediately headed my way. He had on a suit and tie, which were not required with us, and in his lapel was the flag pin he'd been sporting since we won the war against Iraq. Myself, I was wearing a flannel shirt and jeans. The Lord has no dress code, was how I saw it, although I knew Conrad Burns disagreed.

He led with a hard-pumping handshake. "Beautiful morning, but early. Too early. Tell me, how's the mission?"

By "mission," he meant my Sanipure route. The executives in Ohio were big on religious business language. A sale was a "fellowship moment." Recruiting someone to come in under you was known as "spreading abundance," and rising through the ranks was called "ascending."

"It's not so good," I said. I had to tell the truth: Conrad Burns had seen my sales reports. "There've been some problems lately. With the products."

Conrad Burns said, "Yes?" and touched his tie, which was patterned with silver Liberty Bells. I recognized the tie as a Sanipure sales award; ditto his red-white-and-blue enamel flying-eagle cuff links. He stood there, a glittering tribute to our nation, his bowling-pin-shaped body blocking all escape routes.

"The laundry detergent's the main one," I said. "The label says it's hypoallergenic, but customers tell me it makes their skin itch."

"We've heard that one before," said Conrad Burns. "Please go on, though. Criticism interests me." His wife, who was standing next to us, turned away to chat with a man whom I knew she didn't like.

"Can't we do this later?" I said, and I looked around for someone to rescue me. Lucas was at the front door, holding it open for some of the old people. I lifted my head, but he didn't seem to see me—too busy helping a lady in a wheelchair.

Conrad Burns said, "Here's a tip. Never be afraid to speak your mind about the product—unless, of course, you think you're wrong. On the other hand, look to your own self first. The product will never please everyone, but unless you please yourself . . ." He gave me his patented searching stare, the one that I knew he'd been coached in at his monthly distributors' workshops. I held up fairly well to it, I thought, blinking only once.

But one blink was enough with Conrad Burns. "You're troubled," he said. "What's the matter?"

"I told you. The laundry detergent—"

"The real one."

I said, "I'm considering giving up my route." The fact was I hadn't considered it till then, but I wanted to shock Conrad Burns, whose unshakable faith in Sanipure had always seemed vaguely blasphemous to me. Also, I needed to focus on Kim now.

"It sounds like you're giving up, period," he said. He looked me up and down. "If I were you, I'd think again.

Sanipure forgives our lapses, Weaver, but not indefinitely."

He turned away and rejoined his wife. I went to the men's room to wet-comb my hair and check that my collar was straight. I had always felt sloppy around Conrad Burns, and though I no longer liked him or respected him, the thought of his disapproval frightened me. The church was my family, the Body of Christ, and Conrad Burns, despite his many faults, was as much a part of it as anyone.

Mrs. Parshall was right: her grandniece, Melissa, showed up for services. The two of them chose a pew a few rows up from mine, the pew some people called "the display case" because it was where our single women sat. A man named Peter Gluck, overweight, divorced, and not our most trustworthy Christian, stopped beside the pew and said hello. Melissa slid over, making room for him. He was about to squeeze in next to her when Lucas, who kept an eye out for trouble and showed up out of nowhere when he saw some, tapped him on the shoulder and loaded him down with a stack of programs. Peter left to distribute the programs and Lucas sat down with Melissa.

The hymns sounded thin and wobbly, too few voices, but the sermon that morning was better than average. Reverend Spannring's appointment at the airport forced him to compress, to cut out the usual long-winded stories about his days on a Ford assembly line. He could relate his old job to anything, from Christians' need to work together to the terrible price we pay for sloth. But today he spoke plainly, nothing automotive, and I wished that Kim was there with me to hear him. I had telephoned her the night before and offered to swing by and pick her up, but she had said she'd be tired in the morning and that I should visit her after the service. Though I knew it was still too early to push her, I felt a little angry at myself for letting her off the hook so easily.

The chapel smelled of soapy Sunday flesh, of talcum powder and menthol shaving cream, as Reverend Spannring cleared his throat and steadied his spread-out hands on the rostrum. Mothers hushed their babies, men sat straighter.

"The world is doomed," said Reverend Spannring, "because it is the world."

He stood there, shaking lightly, face gone white.

"The world is doomed because it is the world. This earth was not meant to house us forever, but to be destroyed and taken from us. It is not heaven, but heaven's waiting room. We get bored here, we get tired, we get restless. We want to be entertained while we wait—read magazines, have 'love affairs,' dine on 'gourmet' food. We want the world to be pleasing in itself instead of for what it leads to: a better life with Christ. Because we're weak, we want this. Because we are decayed inside. Paul writes, in his letter to the . . ."

Behind me, I heard crying, an outbreak of sniffly, snot-rattling sobs. I turned around. It was little Billy Gruen. His parents, Bob and Rita, recovering gamblers who treated Sunday chapel as their personal baby-sitting service, were nowhere in sight. I made what I thought was a face of reassurance and Billy Gruen cried harder.

"In a world we are bound to lose and see destroyed," continued Reverend Spannring, "how should we live? What stance should we take? I played a board game the other day: Trivial Pursuit. What a revealing name, I thought. A game of questions that do not matter and answers that matter less. 'Which child star rode National

Velvet to fame?' 'Who was the Iron Man to his Yankee teammates?' "

I heard Billy Gruen say, "Lou Gehrig." All around me, disapproving heads turned. I picked at a spot on the hymnal in my lap.

". . . But there is only one iron man: Christ."

There was a chapel-wide sigh of agreement.

"And life is not a trivial pursuit. *Unless we make it one.*"

I looked back up. Reverend Spannring's mouth was open, holding the note. Melissa, up in front, was whispering in Lucas's ear and getting grave nods in response. The man beside me was saying, "Amen." The reverend's point was corny, in a way, but it was our point, born in our chapel, paid for out of our own pockets. Not to let it sink in would be wasteful.

The wrap-up was short and forceful. "Resist! Resist the world! Be world-resisters. Do not be diverted by trivial pursuits. I'm speaking to our youth, particularly. Believe me, I've seen the popular T-shirt: 'Life is a bitch, and then you die.' Well, perhaps, life *is* a little bitchy, but what comes after isn't death. It's glory. Life is a struggle, and then you triumph. So climb to the top of this heap of decay and sing hallelujah!"

There were thirty or forty loud "Hallelujahs" and one insistent, small "Lou Gehrig."

In the lobby after the service, Lucas said, "You remember Melissa."

"I do," I said. "It's good to have you back."

Melissa said, "Thank you," and pinched her throat. I remembered it as a habit of hers, always touching her throat when she spoke, as if her voice box were manually operated.

"Weaver here," said Lucas, "has made some great gains in the Lord this year. Great strides. He's quite the Good Samaritan. Quite the shepherd of little lost sheep."

I did not appreciate all this, particularly the "sheep" part. Lucas, it seemed, had found out about Kim and wanted me to know it. One aspect of his surveillance mania was posing as somewhat omniscient himself.

I turned to Melissa: "How was San Francisco?"

I knew the answer from looking at her face. Her nose had a bumpy red rash around it, as though from a permanent allergy. Her curly, dark hair had thinned considerably, with the patchiness found in old bearskin rugs. Her eyes were not the eyes I remembered but looked like transplants from someone who had died, a car-wreck victim who'd checked the box on her driver's license.

"I liked California," Melissa said. "It's nice. All the nice beaches. They're peaceful."

"Beaches remind me of beachheads," Lucas said. "I'm afraid I can't relax on them."

I smiled but decided not to laugh.

Melissa let go of her throat and said flatly, "I want to fight abortion. I told Lucas. Abortion is just destroying us, it ruins girls' insides. Men have no idea."

"I'm sure you're right," I said. A touchy moment. Clearly, Melissa had had one out there—an abortion of her own. The Conscience Squad's ranks were filled with such women, though few of them admitted it out loud. You could see it on their faces, though: the strain.

Lucas said, "Ours is a people cause, Melissa. Everyone can make a contribution. Weaver here contributes more than most, but Weaver's tireless. He's a superhero."

"Lucas, you're being a jerk," I said. I didn't care that Melissa could hear—she wouldn't remember any of this, except that two men had paid attention to her. "I want to know what your point is," I said.

"Only this: you do too much. You do things you're not assigned to do. Running after damsels in distress."

Melissa said, "Excuse me, I want to talk to Peter now."

Lucas watched her go and shook his head. "Lost in boyland," he said. "She'll never learn." He squared off his stance and faced me. "You missed a meeting last week. I called your place."

"What meeting?" I said. "It wasn't on the schedule."

"Not all meetings are on the schedule. Some meetings just come up. Where were you?"

I told him: at Kim's. I had nothing to hide.

"Come out to my car," he said. "We need to talk."

The car, which I hadn't seen before, was a beat-up Plymouth station wagon that appeared to have forded muddy rivers on its way to church. Though Lucas must have bought the car that week (he changed vehicles almost as often as he changed motel rooms), the interior was already a mess. Potato-chip fragments covered the floor. The seats were littered with newspapers, Coke cans, Styrofoam coffee cups. In the back I saw a rolled-up sleeping bag and a ripped-open bag of disposable razors. Packets of moist towelettes were everywhere, and I wondered if Lucas bathed anymore or merely swabbed off whichever body part was temporarily most offensive.

We got into the car and sat there for a moment, silent, looking out through the bug-spotted windshield. Reverend Spannring rushed past us, waving, dragging a suitcase on rumbling metal casters. Lucas leaned over in front of me and opened the glove compartment. Inside it I saw maps, pill bottles, a saw-backed hunting knife, and Lucas's pistol—a silver .38. I had asked him once to let me shoot the gun, but he had said I wasn't qualified, that I would have to complete a course first. Lucas belonged to the NRA and liked to say that firearm freedom depends on firearm safety.

He popped a couple Prozacs, chewing them for faster action. His eyes were on the rearview as he said: "You have time to drive somewhere? Take a little drive?"

I checked my watch. Kim was expecting me. "Actually—" I said.

Lucas glanced in his side mirror. "We can do this here, I guess." He spread his knees and reached beneath the seat, coming up with a large manila envelope. He handed it across to me. "Open that and tell me what you think. This is what you missed last week, while you were off with your girlfriend."

"She's not my girlfriend," I said.

"Semantics."

The top sheet was a list of Squad members' names and phone numbers, the one I myself had compiled earlier that month. Beneath it was our August calendar of meetings, including the annual softball game. Next was a stapled-together stack of flimsy computer paper that looked like the script of a play. Printed across the top of each page was a date and a time.

"Telephone conversations," said Lucas. He took back the papers, stuffed them in the envelope, and slid it back under the seat. "The membership list and calendar aren't my chief concerns—they're only minor leaks. The wiretaps, though . . ."

"What wiretaps?"

Lucas said, "You saw them. Those were wiretap transcripts. Government or private doesn't matter. Old Lucas is drawing more scrutiny than ever, that's the bottom line." He tipped back his head against the headrest and drummed his fingers on the steering wheel. He jutted out his lower jaw, grinding the hinge. A stress machine.

"Show me the papers again," I said. "I didn't get a good look at them."

"Weaver, you can't imagine how it feels. You cannot imagine. The opposite of safe."

Lucas sat up straight and turned the ignition key. He turned it slowly, dramatically, as if he expected to trigger a bomb. I was starting to have real doubts about him. All that junk food. The antidepressants.

"This time the threat is serious," he said. "The same special interests who got Judge Bork are after me now. They're cornered, they know it, so they're turning vicious. Basically, they hate all leaders. Total anarchists."

"You're sure you're not dreaming this up?" I said.

"Weaver, you'll have to trust me."

There was a rap on the driver's side window: Melissa. Lucas rolled it down and she leaned in. "My aunt's going home with the Pattersons," she said. "We're fine until tonight."

Melissa walked past the front of the car, coming around to my side. Lucas used the rearview mirror to shoot me a look of military warning. "I'm taking the girl out to lunch," he said. "It's strictly a welcome-back thing. Social. It doesn't have to be national news."

Crossing the parking lot to my car, I remembered I'd promised to pray for Lucas and that I hadn't done it yet.

Now I wasn't sure I wanted to.

Seven

Kim said, "I thought about calling the cops, but it wasn't really a burglary. Loring has a key."

I leaned against the doorframe, blinking at the damage.

"It was like this when I got back from the store. I thought you should see it," she said. "He did a pretty thorough job for only having half an hour." She swept an arm around the room, a TV model displaying game-show prizes. "Totaled," she said. "One hundred percent."

It was closer to ninety-eight percent: one of Kim's plants remained in its pot, and the pot still hung from its ceiling hook. Everything else had been trashed. Foam-rubber stuffing boiled from the sofa. The television lay facedown, the back of its cabinet ripped clean off. Cassettes with all their tape spooled out lay in drifts against the bathroom door, which hung from its frame by a single splintered hinge. A bulbless metal standard lamp had apparently served as a club and a spear, batting knickknacks off the shelves and gouging holes in the walls. The destruction had a science-fiction feel, as if some hungry Martian robot had feasted on Kim's apartment, then thrown away the bones.

"See over there?" said Kim. "He pissed in here. That curvy dark line on the wall, that's Loring's urine."

I looked at the spot and saw my Bible, its pages fanned and torn, lying on a heap of broken dishes. I went to the Bible and picked it up, holding it by a corner of the cover. "How do you know who did this?" I said.

"I recognize the urine smell. Loring takes lots of B-complex—it gives him this funny smell, like yeast."

The Bible felt strangely heavy; it was soaked. I dropped it on the floor and wiped my hands on my jeans. The filth. The filth that almost drowns you every time you get involved in someone else's life.

Kim stepped past me through the debris. Her movements were giddy, almost pirouettish. Perhaps she had been expecting something like this to happen, and now that it had, she felt relieved. Or maybe she was in shock, whatever shock is.

I watched her pick up a badly cracked vase, examine it for a moment, then let it fall and shatter.

"This Loring," I said. "He's your boyfriend?"

"My paramour," said Kim. "He called himself my paramour. He studies French at the U of M. He's very romantic, very bright. Intense."

"Why do you think he . . . ?"

"The kid," she said.

It's what I did not want to hear. Kim's child, if I could convince her to keep it, would have no father. Or at least no father capable of loving it.

Kim said, "It's this way. He called me last night and asked if I'd had the abortion yet—he must have found out I'd cashed his check—and I said no, not yet, I wanted to think about it some more. And Loring said fine, he'd handle things himself. His family's very wealthy, see; he thinks I got pregnant to force him into marriage."

"Did you?" The words had just popped out. I wasn't proud of them, but there they were.

Kim's tone was thoughtful. "Not consciously, no. Sure, I had fantasies—honeymoon, big house—but I have those about every guy I date. I wasn't even Loring's girlfriend, really, just a part-time fuck. Fact is, I think he's engaged. I'm sure of it. You have to understand: Loring's good looking, flattering to be with. When he told me one night he could feel my diaphragm, I cut it up and flushed it down the toilet. He really had me going. Christ . . ."

"I'm sorry I brought it up," I said. "This Loring sounds like a terrible person."

Kim pushed some glass around with her sandal. "I guess that maybe depends on what you're used to."

We didn't bother to clean the place up. We wouldn't have known where to start. I tried to persuade Kim to call the police, explaining that her insurance company might require a report from them, but Kim said she had no insurance. I asked if the building's landlord had a policy, and Kim said she didn't know. She wasn't even sure she had a lease. The situation was so confused I got a headache discussing it. Kim said there was some Tylenol in the bathroom cabinet, but when she came back from looking for it, she said that all her medicines were floating in the toilet bowl.

I asked her if she would like some dinner, and she said yes, she needed to eat.

We drove across town to what Kim said was her favorite restaurant. It was called McClancey's, a fake English pub with plaster oak beams decorated with plaster coats of arms. The place was crowded with people in their twenties drinking foamy dark beer from frosted mugs and tossing peanut shells on the floor. I had been to my share of pickup bars before, and this was a pickup bar, I decided. The waitresses wore lacy, low-cut tops that shoved up their breasts in that old-fashioned way. Their feet were bound in pointy, antique boots. When people say that the old days were moral, I wonder how they know. From what I have seen of the old days, they were even more corrupt than these days.

The hostess, whose breasts bulged higher than anyone else's, wrote my last name in a large leather book and told us to wait at the bar for a table. We squeezed in next to some middle-aged men whose haircuts and outfits were sad imitations of the younger men's.

I asked Kim what she wanted to drink, hoping, for the baby's sake and hers, it wasn't a beer.

"A diet Coke," she said.

I ordered diet Cokes for both of us.

"I used to come here with Loring," said Kim. "Sometimes by myself, when he was with his fiancée. The men can be awfully crude, but you get used to it. It's sort of fun to put them in their place."

As if to demonstrate, she winked in the backbar mirror

at a man in a fancy sport coat drinking a tall blue cocktail. When the man nodded back, she gave him the finger.

He gave it back to her.

Completely pointless.

As we finished our Cokes, Kim shelled a peanut and set it by my glass, then shelled another and popped it in her mouth. "If you're wondering why I'm not crushed about the break-in, it's because I see the bright side: no more Loring. I can't believe I ever let him touch me. Talk about not respecting yourself."

I said, "Will you miss him?"

Kim almost choked on her peanut. "You're kidding. That's like saying would you miss a sickness. My only regret is I didn't bite it off when I had the chance."

A few minutes later, when the hostess called our names, Kim started sobbing and we had to leave.

The sacredness of human life, the destruction of American society, and why Kim should take a couple of weeks to consider options besides abortion. Those were the topics I hoped to bring up as we sat in my car an hour or two later, eating our burgers and french fries and trying to bring a confusing day to a meaningful ending.

We were parked in a Burger King parking lot, having just come back from Kim's apartment, where we had found what remained of her belongings piled in the hallway. The urine smell had turned to ammonia, and we could hear the landlord and another man talking inside Kim's living room. The men sounded angry, and Kim got scared. She said her landlord was a vicious man who sometimes used pit bulls to evict bad tenants and that he would hold her responsible for what her boyfriend had done to his property. She said she could never go back there. I asked her if she had a girlfriend she could stay with and she said, "I've never had close woman friends. I guess I don't pause long enough between boyfriends."

There wasn't any choice: I offered to let Kim stay with me, at least for a little while, until she got back on her feet. I said I could give her some money, if she needed it; not a lot, but some.

Kim said, "That's so sweet of you. Maybe I can pay you back sometime. I don't know when I'll be able to, but . . ."

"You don't understand," I said. "It's a gift. I don't expect repayment."

"Why is that?"

I looked at her as if the answer were obvious, although I had no idea what it was. I started trying things. "Because you're in trouble," I said. "Because you need a friend. You have a decision to make. A big one. I want to help you do what's right."

"So it's not just because you maybe sort of *like me*? I mean if you hate me, and this is just a *duty* . . ."

"I like you a lot." I had to say it. I decided that I could figure out later whether I really meant it.

"And what about my condition?" said Kim. "Physically, I mean. You're not going to climb all over me about it? Because if you do, I'll leave. I don't respond well to pressure."

"Fine," I said. "But I don't think you would have phoned me that night if you thought you had all the answers. Don't you agree you had some second thoughts?" I was applying a basic tenet from Sanipure's training manual: Always meet resistance with a question.

"Maybe you're right," Kim said. "Maybe I'm confused."

There was a look of real pain on her face, her major features suddenly in combat, and I thought she was going to cry again.

We ate our burgers and listened to the radio. Kim had turned on "American Top Forty." What upset me the most were the drums. Their beat was not a human beat but demonically rapid and harsh. The lyrics were almost as bad. They promised a state of freedom and excitement they could not deliver, but Kim seemed to believe in them, so I kept my feelings to myself. There was so much I wanted to say to her. I wanted to tell her about God's plan for her, about the peace that can fill the soul when you have done your best to empty it. I wanted to tell her that evil is real and possession is not just a thing in the movies—what else could account for the boy from Hidden Planet who went out one night to the discos with a razor blade? He cut up his arms in a club called Crocodile and spun around on the dance floor, spraying blood on people and laughing. A lot of the people around him laughed, too.

Instead, I said, "Kim, are you happy?"

"Not especially. Not tonight." She lifted the bun off her burger and rearranged the pickle slices, pushing them around with her finger. She bit the corner off a ketchup packet and squeezed the ketchup onto her patty in a zigzag pattern. "Seeing how I lost my home today," she said, "I'm doing pretty well, though, don't you think?"

"In general," I said. "Are you happy in general?"

"I am, as a matter of fact." She reached across my lap and stole a french fry. "I like my work."

"You quit your job, though."

"Not that," she said. "My cards."

I nodded and sucked on my straw, draining the last of

my large-size orange soda. I had forgotten about Kim's cards; I hoped that she would forget about them, too. They were not sinful, exactly, just unhelpful.

"Mind if I turn down the music?" I said as I turned it down. The song that had just come on compared making love to being lost in space, and I couldn't take it. I closed my Styrofoam burger box and stuffed it back in the bag. I thought back to when I had worked at McDonald's and how, at night, when we put out the garbage, homeless people would gather near the Dumpsters and fight one another for the cold Big Macs. Eventually, we constructed a fence and padlocked the gate. Our fallen world.

I held out the box of ketchup-tipped french fries. Kim took some and said, "I read your Bible."

I looked at her and sat up straighter.

"Not the whole thing," she said. "Just the Psalms and Proverbs. I enjoyed them."

"The greatest poetry ever," I said, happy for a chance to brag for God. "Even a lot of atheists admit that. Literature professors."

"They're very inspiring," she said.

But that was all. Kim finished her burger, chewing with her eyes closed, and the subject died. I let it die. I started the car and pulled out into traffic, intending to stop at a Safeway on the way to my place. It was time to get Kim on a healthy diet. She needed green salads, oatmeal, orange juice. She needed that solid physical foundation. I asked her to keep an eye out for a giant S.

We still hadn't seen one when Kim said, "Pull over. I think it's an emergency."

I sat in the car and watched her throw up in some cattails next to the road. At first the heaves were delicate, like coughs; I rolled up the window to spare her the embarrassment of knowing I could hear them. Then her body began to shake and buck, a rolling motion that spread from her shoulders and down her back and into her hips. I did not get out and help her because I believed I knew what was happening and that it was something I shouldn't interfere with, something Kim would have to face alone.

When she returned to the car, her tight yellow sweatshirt was spotted with food, and I could smell stomach acid on her breath. That she'd vomited when she had did not surprise me: I took it as a sign. Sometimes, when the Lord first enters you, horrible things are cast out of the body, making room for Him.

It happens all the time.

Eight

THE YEAR BEFORE I WAS BAPTIZED, WHEN THE ALCOHOL, MUSIC, and drugs still had me, I went to a pair of free lectures at a local community college. The flier announcing the lectures (I found it tucked under my windshield wiper when I left work at McDonald's one night) promised that, by attending both sessions, people could be set free from their addictions. Smoking, gambling, anger, defeatism— all of these were listed as addictions, along with drugs and alcohol. I finished reading the flier and wondered if I really needed such a general cure.

But I knew I needed something, so I went. I sat at the back of the hall in case I felt like leaving early. The air had a sharp disinfectant smell; the walls of the room were aquarium green. It made me feel hopeless just being in there, and I thought of the one AA meeting I'd gone to. That had been a sad room, too, with the same queasy smells and awful paint. I decided that it was a law of nature: the ugly rooms attract the ugly people.

On the blackboard above the lectern it said: "Feel free to take notes," but I did not have a pencil. The man who sat down beside me had an extra, but said he needed paper. His face was a wreck. Exploded capillaries. A film on his eyes like spoiled milk, something cheesy pooling in the corners. I asked around and got some paper and offered to take notes for both of us. The man thanked me profusely, then buried his trembling hands in his pockets and kept them there, under restraint, throughout the lecture.

The first part of the lecture was a slide show, and the very first slide was of galaxies and planets. The speaker, whose face I couldn't see (he had taken the mike in darkness), spoke these words: "Herald the new age of freedom! It is real and it is here!" The slide clicked over; two bodies filled the screen. Two naked bodies, a man's and a woman's, their arms raised high to gather in the whirling suns and planets. The bodies were silvery, almost transparent, except for the very tops of the heads, which gave off dazzling purple rays. Looking at them made me dizzy; I'd drunk some beer while driving over and couldn't focus right. I shut my eyes and still saw purple.

"Perfected Aquarian beings," the voice said. "What all of us in this room can choose to be."

After maybe ten more slides and heraldings, the lights came on and the speaker was revealed as a man in his thirties with surfer-boy blond hair. He introduced himself as Peter Spain and said he had been a doctor once, a clinical psychiatrist. I wrote in my notes that he did not seem old enough. He went on to say he had quit his practice when he discovered his skills were worthless. *Worthless skills*, I wrote. He told us that doctors have no idea how to heal man's most serious ailments, and that they know this but will not admit it, except to one another.

"The money was great, the golf was fantastic, but medicine was a lie," said Peter Spain. "I simply couldn't go on with the lie."

A few people clapped, the ones who clap at anything.

"And then I discovered Ergonics, the practical science of mind," said Peter Spain. "A science I wish to share with you tonight, and one that I guarantee will change your lives."

But Ergonics itself was not mentioned again that night, only its miraculous results. Photographic memory. Success with the opposite sex. Self-confidence. Mastery over destructive habits. More slides were shown: of hand-holding couples walking on a beach, of old people playing Frisbee in a park, of businessmen in limousines and female marathon runners sprinting ahead of the pack. "Total exaltation," Peter Spain said, filling up the darkness with his voice. "Physical, spiritual, even financial. I deserve it, you deserve it—the only question is, how do we start? The only question is, what are we waiting for?"

I waited, pencil ready, for the secret. Then the lights came on again. Peter Spain had vanished and a dark-haired young woman was standing in his spot. "Lecture two, 'Ergonics Revealed,' will be held tomorrow night. Those who attend will also receive, completely free of charge, a personal Ergon analysis conducted by counselors like myself. So be here, and remember: Aquarian rebirth is up to you!"

I arrived an hour late for lecture two. I didn't want to see more slides or hear more promises—I wanted the analysis. I wanted the woman to test my Ergons and tell me, in her beautiful clear voice, how I could join this new age of freedom where everyone looked like a movie star without having movie stars' personal problems. I showed up stoned and a little bit drunk to make the test realistic.

I wanted a true and accurate analysis that would measure me at my worst.

I didn't get the dark-haired young woman. I got an older one, not so attractive, who was almost as tall as my mother the businesswoman. I followed her down a hallway to another part of the building, where we sat in a booth on two folding chairs behind a plastic shower curtain. The woman started shooting questions at me, looking me hard in the eye while writing in shorthand in a spiral notebook. The questions were all different kinds: Do you smoke? Do you like to watch violence? What are your fears? Do you masturbate? Do you eat foods that aren't good for you? Why? *What led you to these lectures?*

If I was slow to give an answer, the woman would snort and roll her eyes as if I were the stupidest person in the world. Whatever I had been about to say would get backed up inside my head as the woman fired off another question, each one more embarrassing and private. Soon, my heart began to pound and the light in the booth went flickery, strobish. The woman's voice was the only steady presence. At some point, the questions became accusations: "You failure. You pitiful fuck-up. You drunk. You're an animal, not even human. You're brain-dead!"

I found myself crying, apologizing, asking forgiveness for things I'd never done and ways I'd never been.

After perhaps ten minutes of this, the woman put down her notebook and held my hand and said, "You're doing it. Let yourself do it. Ride the lifestream."

By the time the session ended, I was calm. My arms and legs felt heavy, warm. Over and over, I thanked the woman, who had become so beautiful to me I wanted to stay in the booth with her forever. She told me to go to a room across the hall, where I would receive my personalized report and be offered a chance to continue with Ergonics. I asked her if I would see her again. She smiled and said that that was up to me.

The room across the hall was not crowded. I recognized some people from the lecture, but I also saw that a lot of them had left. The man with the wreck of a face had stayed, though; he was standing in front of a card table piled high with paperback books. I saw a dark stain on his trouser leg; apparently he had wet himself in the course of his analysis. I looked around for Peter Spain, but all I saw were some autographed photos displayed on another card table. People were paying money for the pictures, opening their wallets. I was wondering whether I should do the same when a college-age boy in a suit approached, asked my name, and handed me my report: a sheet of yellow paper covered with wavy, complicated graph lines.

"This is your key to progress," said the boy. "You can't move to higher levels without it. If you'd like us to interpret the results, there will be a fee of ninety dollars."

I looked at the wavy lines, confused.

"Believe me," the boy said, "it's worth it. Think of what hospitals charge. Psychiatrists. All we're doing is covering our costs. Mr. Spain was not cheap to get here—he's one of the highest Ergon masters."

I thought about this and said, "I'd like to talk to that lady again. The one from my session. I need to see her now."

"Counselor Sherman is gone. She's back in Minneapolis, at the Center. I'm sure that if you want more sessions, though, she will be glad to conduct them."

I pictured her moving red lips, her tongue. The movements of her eyebrows when she cursed me. I saw myself on my knees in front of her, confessing to every crime. I touched my wallet. I could pay for another session right now and see her tomorrow, after work. Something good would happen then, I knew it. For money, mere money, I could have the Answer.

I turned then to look at the boy and saw a demon.

He lacked the hooves and horns you read about in books, but I knew it was him: the Dark One. His high, curving cheekbones and smooth, tanned skin were like a shop-window mannequin's, that dead. The color seemed to have drained from his eyes. They were gray, staring, bottomless, blank, fallen eyes whose pupils played scenes of heaven upside down—a place where the angels looked like Peter Spain and there was money and health and power and no one who could hurt you whom you could not laugh off. Also, a beautiful woman. To bow before, to touch. To frighten you and excite you, over and over, until you just dissolved . . .

I took a step back from the sight. I didn't run. I knew it wouldn't help to run. You would run and get tired and he would catch up. You had to stand and look into those eyes, at all they had to offer, then show in your own eyes that you did not accept.

I handed the boy my report and said, "No thank you. I'm smarter than this. The New Age doesn't interest me."

Immediately, I could see him grow weaker. His body, his physical body, seemed to shrink. He offered to waive the ninety-dollar fee if I would come down to the Center that night and meet with some "very advanced, special people." I would be served a free meal and shown more slides. Counselor Sherman would read my report and interpret it herself.

I said, "No."

"No is never an answer. No negates. No creates blockage."

I turned and left the room.

I went to my car and sat there, shaking. I lit a joint then put it out, then lit it again. I watched it burn. I started the car and drove for an hour, ending up at a bar; I felt I deserved a drink for my courage. Three girls were dancing topless on a stage. I cashed my paycheck and went to the stage and threw some dollar bills at them. They grinned and wiggled, showing me their parts, and some men at a nearby table started hooting. They bought me a beer and I sat down with them. They said they were part owners of the bar and asked me if I would like to meet the dancers.

That is how it works with Satan. He is in front of you and behind. When you think you have turned your back on Evil, that is when you are facing it again.

I woke up inside my car the next morning, parked at a shopping center, all cut up, with no idea how I had got there. There were bruises and scrapes on the backs of my hands and on my cheeks and legs. I looked around at the parking lot and saw the crowds of early Christmas shoppers, fathers and mothers wheeling carts of gifts across the snowy blacktop. Children were opening car doors for their parents, being extra good.

My wallet was not in my coat.

I smelled like blood.

I remembered all this the night Kim came to stay with me, after I put her to bed in my room and turned off the light and shut the door. I lay on the sofa and thought: *She's safe in there.* But then I thought back to the slides of New Age lovers, to the demon and Counselor Sherman and the dancers, and I did not know if I was safe where I was. Two years in the Lord is no time at all: you can slip in an instant. A woman can make you. And then you are part of her again, a nothing, and you may as well not have been born. You may as well have never left the darkness.

Nine

THE PHONE RANG AT SEVEN O'CLOCK THE NEXT MORNING. I was already awake, lying on the sofa with my eyes shut, listening to a tape called *New Beginnings* and trying to stay on top of a thought that was threatening to run away with me.

The thought had a slight connection to the tape. The tape was a speech on Christian conversion given by the Reverend Armand Dale, host of the cable talk show "Positions." The show aired Thursday nights at eight, during the weekly Conscience Squad meeting. I would tape it on my VCR and play it back on Friday evenings, a habit that kept me at home and out of trouble.

The show's format was simple and to me, brilliant: Reverend Dale would interview a celebrated figure, someone from sports or politics or movies, concerning his or her deepest beliefs, religious and philosophical. He didn't let guests lie to him or hide behind clichés and pleasantries. Reverend Dale was a graduate of the Harvard Divinity School, with firm, intelligent features and vocal chords of hardened alloy. If a guest played games with the reverend, whether the guest was a Super Bowl halfback or a U.S. congressman, there was never any question who would win.

What Reverend Dale too often found out was that a guest had no beliefs at all, or none worth mentioning. I remember one "Positions" where a muscle-man movie star claimed to believe, at bottom, in himself. Reverend Dale pursued the matter: "Which self? The one with the thirty-inch biceps, or the self which sought to overcome its shame by building up such arms?" The movie star said he had never been ashamed, and Reverend Dale said, "Then it must be fear. Why would a man of average height and weight turn himself into a monster of muscle unless he was either ashamed or terrified? What are you afraid of?"

"Not a thing."

"Then, sir, you truly are a monster."

The *New Beginnings* cassette tape was nowhere near as dramatic as "Positions." It suffered from too much chilly scripture-quoting. It explained why a person *had to* convert but not why he *should*. I listened to it, thinking: *What if Kim chooses to keep her child but refuses to come to Christ—will the rescue have been worth it? Or will it just produce a newborn corpse, alive in the flesh but dead in the spirit?* Then the thought got away from me, turned horrible. Images from the Conscience Squad pamphlets, of tiny aborted body parts and ghostly sonograms, flashed

75

through my mind. A spirit army of unborn children, nameless and invisible, but out there somewhere nonetheless. With wings. I imagined the babies had wings, that they could fly; millions of screaming, mutilated angels swooping back and forth above the earth. But why, if there were so many of them, could only a few people hear them, such as me? And how could I be so sure they were screaming?

Maybe they were singing.

Maybe it was bliss for them to be set free so young.

That's when the telephone rang, and it was my mother the businesswoman.

"Good," she said. "You're not in prison."

"Hello, Margaret. What are you talking about?"

"This Boone," my mother said, "this Lucas Boone. I saw the whole business on 'Eyewitness News.' I thought you might be with him."

"I never watch 'Eyewitness News,' " I said. "It's biased and it's not about my life. 'Eyewitness News' is a clever plot to convince us that all the important events are happening somewhere else, to other people, at the same time we're literally dying in our beds."

My mother said, "You sound ghastly, Weaver. Programmed or something. Brainwashed."

"I try."

"Well, at least you weren't actually *with* the fellow, actually on *the scene*," my mother said. "I suppose it could be worse."

"On what scene?"

My mother described the incident as if it shocked her deeply, though of course it could not have pleased her more. She did not approve of Lucas Boone. The year I joined the Conscience Squad, she asked to meet him to find out what I saw in him. The three of us went to a diner for coffee and had a polite, angry talk about free will. We agreed that everyone had free will and that some of us used it more wisely than others. We agreed that abortion was not the highest use, though my mother said it was not the lowest either. Then she asked Lucas if I was using my free will or being absorbed by his. He lost it. He asked her if she was proud of herself for raising a son who had ended up unconscious on a men's-room floor, choking on vomit and stolen pain pills. A son who had tried to kill himself (this was not precisely true) and had to be Heimlich-maneuvered back to life. My mother asked me if this had really happened, and when I said, "Basically, yes," she started crying. She said it was all my dead father's fault.

"Weaver, you would have hated him," she said. "You would have fought nonstop, you're so alike. You would have learned a lot about yourself." She made a big show of drying her eyes, inking up several napkins with mascara and piling them on her saucer like blighted white carnations. "Instead, you fought with me," she said, "a woman, and didn't learn a thing."

It must have been sweet revenge for her to see the "Eyewitness News" story and be the first one to tell me about it. She spoke meticulously, setting forth the facts. Lucas Boone had been shot, she said, superficially wounded while sitting in his car in Como Park. The woman who shot him—no name; the police were not releasing her identity—claimed that Lucas had tried to rape her, and she had used his gun in self-defense. I asked my mother if charges had been filed and if the news had described the woman. She said she wasn't sure about the charges, but that the woman was thirty-two years old and attended the same church as Lucas Boone.

I fell silent, thinking of Melissa.

My mother said, "This surprises you? I thought I'd wised you up about these loonies."

I didn't give her the satisfaction.

"Oh, there's something else," my mother said. She was gloating now. "The police searched the car and found a book on bombs. Apparently, your guru, Mr. Boone—"

"Correction," I said. "He's not my guru, Margaret. I've told you a hundred times: I washed my own brain. I had to—it was filthy."

My mother coughed and laughed, then said, "Forgive me. This dark, sinful background you insist on having just strikes me as hilarious sometimes. You're very attached to it, aren't you? This notion of having survived the devil's clutches?"

Again, I felt no need to answer her, or even fully listen. I thought of the manila envelope under Lucas's carseat and of our conversation after church. "The media's not reporting things," I said. "Lucas carries a gun because he is probably under surveillance. Also, he's a Navy veteran, which explains the bomb book. Plus, I happen to know the girl involved. She isn't exactly the Virgin—"

I decided not to go into it—Melissa's reputation. Eventually, it would all come out, and Lucas would be cleared. The group would pray for him, night and day. We would wear out our knees on the cold church-basement floor, and my mother would learn the truth: that if anyone had molested anyone, it had been Melissa. She shouldn't have been there—she should have known. Should have known that Lucas wasn't strong now.

I heard my mother sigh. She said, "Come home. My store needs a manager—let's discuss it. Everything between us is negotiable. We can go back twenty years, if you want. See a counselor together."

The *New Beginnings* tape ran out then; the speakers hissed static. Through the bedroom door, I could hear Bryant Gumbel on TV, poking fun at the U.S. Congress. Little people tearing down big ones; it had been happening all my life. President Nixon, Pete Rose, Mrs. Reagan, Jimmy Swaggart, everyone. Maybe Lucas was right about the systematic destruction of our leaders. Maybe he was the next one on the list.

"Next time," I said to my mother, "write, don't call. And send an extra check this month. I have some new expenses."

"Forget it."

"I'm taking care of someone. Send the check."

"What will you do if I don't?" my mother said. "What can you do that's worse than what you're doing?"

I was about to provide some graphic examples when Kim appeared in the doorway, wearing only her T-shirt and panties. "I'm hungry," she said. "I dreamed I needed salt." She wandered sleepily past me to the kitchen and started throwing open cabinets. Her tummy had a slight roll above the panties. Her nipples were dark and hard inside the shirt.

My mother said, "You've got a girl there?"

"Yes."

"At least there's that to be thankful for," she said. "At least you still have *instincts*."

Then we hung up on each other.

* * *

Kim went back to bed with a box of saltine crackers. I ran out to the corner store and bought some eggs and orange juice. I left them in the kitchen with a note telling Kim that I'd be back by noon. I drove across St. Paul to Derek Griff's house, resisting the temptation to buy a morning paper on the way. As an attorney and friend of the cause, Derek would have the clearest view of Lucas and Melissa's situation. He would know what had happened, what must be done, and what kind of attitude everyone should take. We would place our trust in Derek, not the media; he was our natural leader now.

When I pulled up in front of the house at 9:15, three or four cars were already in the driveway. I went inside without knocking and followed a beaten-down path in the shag through the TV room to Derek's den, where he was sitting unshaven at his desk, holding the phone receiver to his ear and jotting notes on a yellow legal pad. Conrad Burns looked on from the sofa, his normally shining forehead creased and gray. Next to him sat Terry Bream, a born-again black ex-con whose ministry in the federal prisons had once been featured on "PM Magazine." Terry seemed less concerned with Derek than with choosing a blueberry muffin from the tray someone had set up in front of the sofa. A couple of other members, Janet Sykes and Paula Dorne (they published a newsletter, Mothers United), stood together against the wall, arms crossed. It was hard to tell what they thought of all this.

Derek moved the receiver to his other ear. The ear where it had been was red and mottled. Apparently, he had been on a long time.

"Have a muffin," Terry said. "Paula and Janet went to lots of trouble."

"Thanks, I'm not hungry."

"Some tea, then. Milk and sugar?"

I nodded and said, "Is Lucas okay?"

Terry lifted the china teapot and poured with delicate, four-star formality. "Harmless little scratch," he said. "I hope he's got good medication, though. I don't care where those bullets hit, they *sting*. I'll bet he wished she'd got him through the heart once he felt his armpit."

I took the cup of tea from Terry and shifted my elbow around, experimenting. How did a person get shot in the armpit? What would he have to be doing with his body to be vulnerable from such an angle?

Suddenly, it occurred to me that Lucas might be guilty after all.

Derek said into the phone, "Just a moment, Brian," and turned to face us all, covering the mouthpiece with his hand. "This is a police friend on the line. Lucas is still being questioned, apparently."

Janet said, "What does that mean?"

"That they haven't charged him yet," said Derek. "You and Paula run along now. I promise to call if there's news."

Paula lifted her jacket off a chairback, but Janet didn't budge.

"What's Lucas saying?" Janet asked. "That he didn't do it, right?"

"No. He's being smart," said Derek. "He isn't saying anything."

Janet seemed dissatisfied with this. "And how is the girl?" she said. "No one has even mentioned *her* yet."

"Melissa's at home with her aunt," said Derek. "Physically, she's fine. Mentally, a little shaken up."

Paula touched Janet's arm. "Come on, hon. The men are handling everything."

Derek said, "We are. And thanks for breakfast—that was dear of you."

As soon as the women had gone, Derek concluded his call and put down the phone. He scribbled more notes on the legal pad. Conrad Burns leaned forward, watching him, following every pen stroke with red, shattered eyes. I knew that it didn't matter to him how events turned out. For Conrad, all hope had already been lost. Merely for knowing a could-be rapist, he would be busted in rank by Sanipure. No more free tie tacks and patriotic cuff links.

Looking at him, I made a decision: my selling days were over. No more fellowship moments, no more soap. Sanipure's golden pyramid of infinitely spreading wealth and happiness would have to grow without me.

Derek put the pad in a desk drawer and swiveled around in his leather lawyer's chair. Above him, on the wall, was an autographed photo of Senator Helms next to a framed commendation from his office. I looked at the seal on the commendation and wondered who had stamped it there —the senator himself or an assistant? Maybe such documents weren't so special and anyone who wanted one could get one.

"Here is what we're dealing with," said Derek. "First, though, let me be clear: I'm speaking as our attorney now, not Boone's. I'll talk to him, but I won't represent him. We have to think of ourselves now, of the church. I spoke this morning with Pastor Spannring and his instructions to me were explicit."

Terry tore off a chunk of muffin and dunked it in his tea.

"The first step," said Derek, "is dissolution. The Squad will have to dissolve; fold itself into some other group, perhaps. However this affair comes out, we simply can't survive the bad publicity."

Conrad Burns said, "I agree. No scandals." He looked around at us, hangdog and expectant, as if he were seeking our votes. Terry sipped tea and gave no sign of anything. I stared at the wall, at the commendation. I decided it was a forgery.

Derek said, "Step two is to begin right here, right now, to disassociate ourselves from Boone. The man's a liability. Whatever he did or didn't do last night—it really doesn't matter—his behavior has been bizarre in the extreme."

Terry spread some jam on a muffin. "Bizarre is not a crime. What about semen?"

Derek shook his head. "No ejaculate. No abrasions, either. Which means there was either no penetration or, perhaps, that she was lubricated. Lubrication doesn't mean consent, but that's what his lawyer will try to make it mean. *If* it comes to that."

Conrad Burns stood up off the sofa; suddenly, he looked panicky, frantic. He seemed to have lost control of his hands, which were flopping and flapping like injured baby animals. Terry said, "What is it?" and Conrad said, "We shouldn't be here. This whole situation is none of our business. 'Lubrication'—I'm surprised at us!"

Derek stroked his stubble and was silent for a moment. Everybody looked at him. He said, "Of course, I can try to persuade the girl to drop it—believe me, it's in her interest—but that won't repair the damage to our image."

Terry grinned. "What image? We don't have one." He set down his cup on its saucer, then patted the ends of his mustache with a napkin. He stood and buttoned his coat and said, "Gentlemen, I have souls to save. Excuse me." Conrad followed him out of the den as though being sucked by a draft.

Derek turned to me and said, "Eat up those muffins. I'm going back to bed." On his way out, he hit the light switch, so tired he must have forgotten I was there.

I took down the letter from Senator Helms, read it once or twice, then tossed it in the trash and left the house.

Ten

THEY SAY PREGNANT WOMEN ARE MOODY. THINGS COME OVER them. They smile, then cry. They see a picture of something ordinary—a horse eating grass on a mountainside, say—and shiver and blush and can't explain their feelings. No one can explain their feelings. A gentleman is not supposed to try. You treat a woman with a child inside her the way you would treat a sick or dying person. You forget the words *why* and *no* and only say, *Yes, of course.*

So when Kim said she wanted to leave St. Paul and spend a few days in the country, I asked her where in the country, not why she wanted to go.

"Anywhere with leaves," she said. "It's always calmed me down to look at leaves. I think it's because they're all so different but also all the same."

I told her I understood, and we dropped the subject. We were sitting with trays in front of the TV, eating a spinach lasagna I'd made. I had some basic cooking skills because, growing up in my mother's house, I was the only one who ate real food. My mother subsisted on chocolate diet shakes, nail-building gelatin drinks, and multivitamins. Once in a while, she plopped some yogurt on a lettuce leaf or peeled a carrot. Her cheekbones and ankles, she once informed me, were her finest features, and her diet kept them unusually prominent. My mother was a puritan of bone structure.

Kim, however, liked to eat. No matter what I served her, she always cleaned her plate. By her third or fourth day in my apartment, I had even caught her a couple of times standing lit up in the fridge door late at night, sneaking bites of uncooked hot dog and drinking milk from the carton. Her appetite encouraged me; providing for it was something I could do. The torn-in-half bologna slices in my meat compartment didn't bother me in the least.

What did annoy me, though, was *where* Kim ate: on the sofa in front of the television set. It got me watching TV again, a habit I thought I had broken for good, except for my weekly dose of "Positions" and the odd Twins or Vikings game. TV, I believed, was a waste of time. Every hour a person spent watching it left a gap in the story of his life—the story he would have to tell to God when it came time to justify his deeds. But watching TV was not a deed; it didn't count for or against you. It was nothing.

A life spent watching TV could not be judged; it was beneath God's interest. Such a life would have to be lived over, again and again, until the person *acted*.

But Kim needed company, so I watched. She told me

she liked old movies the best, but I noticed she could not sit through a whole one. When I asked her about this, she said she had lied: old movies were Loring's great love, not hers, and he had made her feel guilty for not appreciating them properly. I was glad to hear this. Old movies bored me, too, especially old comedies. They were all about stupid mistakes. Someone made a stupid mistake, then made a bigger one trying to worm out of it, but in the end the mistakes were all excused, or else, by some odd coincidence, they made the person a millionaire or saved somebody's life.

Just meaningless.

What Kim said she liked best were the cop shows. We watched them every night, and to me they were almost as bad as old comedies. Most of them featured pairs of policemen with opposite characteristics. One cop would have short hair, say, and do things by the book, and the other would have long hair and search people's houses without a warrant. The partners would argue for most of the show, but when they finally faced the criminal, they would come together as a team. It was always that way and never any other, as if there were no other plot in the world.

The show we were watching that night featured an older black cop and a rookie white cop, both women. The old one liked to break the rules and it was the young cop who fussed over warrants. I could not have been more bored, but Kim seemed fascinated. Wearing an old flannel shirt I had lent her, she sat way out on the edge of the sofa, not even looking down at her fork when she used it to cut off hunks of lasagna.

"The old one's going to lose her badge," I said. "The

sergeant's going to confiscate her badge, make her quit the investigation, but she'll disobey and get kidnapped or something. Then the young one will rescue her."

Kim said, "Shush, don't spoil it."

"I'm amazed you don't already know."

"Obviously, I'm not as smart as you."

I watched for a few more minutes, until my predictions started coming true. Then I got up and took away our dishes. I stood in front of the sink for a while, drinking a glass of Nestlé's Quik and thinking: *If all Kim does for the next four weeks is watch TV and eat, she'll have to keep the baby. At the end of the first trimester, state law will tie her hands.* I wondered if that might even be her plan: to slip into some sort of waking coma and let whatever happened happen.

But four weeks was a long time, especially if all we did was sit. In my experience, too much sitting always led to trouble. The saying about idleness was true. I looked at the blue moving glow on Kim's face and knew that as long as she sat there dazed like that she was Satan's plaything.

He had already ruined the Bible for her. Yesterday, I had returned from grocery shopping (Kim showed no interest in leaving the apartment) and had found her propped on her elbows on the floor, reading the Old Testament. "It scares me," she said. "It's so violent. It's *horrible*."

"It's nothing compared to TV," I said. "Those police shows you watch are a hundred times worse."

"Except that the shows aren't real. The Bible's supposed to be real."

Only the Devil makes arguments that clever.

I finished my glass of Quik and sat back down on the

sofa. "I've been thinking about the country," I said. "You mentioned last night that you might like to go there. I think we should visit your parents on their farm."

Kim picked up the remote control and aimed it at the screen but didn't change the channel. "How come you have so much soap in this place? So much skin lotion, all that detergent?"

"Don't touch that stuff," I said. "You'll get a rash. Now, about the country—"

"And how come you hate your mother so much?" Kim was trying everything to keep the subject off herself. "I heard you on the phone with her. You were terrible."

"I do not hate my mother. I love her."

"Whatever. Same difference. At least she supports you."

"The money's a bribe."

"You spend it, though."

I had had enough of this. I was not the one in trouble here, the one who had screwed up her life out of sheer irresponsibility and foolishness. "Don't you think you'll feel better," I said, "once you've told your family just what's happening?"

Kim flipped through the channels, saying nothing.

"It's up to you," I said.

I knew it was the only way, though. We had to get out of St. Paul. The apartment was getting too crowded, too close. The day I returned from the meeting at Derek's, I noticed that Kim had tidied up the place. My pictures hung straighter, the sofa was lintless, my desk was a planned executive system. Tracts and pamphlets bound in rubber bands occupied the lower left-hand drawer. The next drawer up was for money matters: checkbook, bank book, receipts, and an envelope full of loose change that Kim must have found by digging in the armchair. Letters received and letters to go out lay on the blotter, corners squared. The topmost note in the out pile ("Dear Columbia Records: In regard to the rock act Reich Warp and their new 'hit album' *Most Precious Blood Bath . . .*") was angry-sounding and personal, and I hoped Kim hadn't read it. There were other things, too, I wished she hadn't touched. A silver bikini-girl Zippo lighter, which my mother said had belonged to my father. A stack of gory war comics left over from my high-school days that I was holding on to in case the series got valuable. A pair of novelty boxer shorts with the words *Beware of Dog* printed over the fly. A girlfriend named Joni who tended bar downtown had given me the shorts three years ago—her sad idea of a Valentine—and I had completely forgotten they existed. I found them in my sock drawer, neatly folded.

But Kim's nosy cleaning was not the only thing getting on my nerves. Lucas Boone's picture had been in all the papers—a grainy black-and-white close-up that not only made him look guilty, but remorseless. The articles had referred to him as the "alleged pro-life rapist," and though the coverage had petered out after last Monday morning (Melissa had dropped the charges, it seemed), I was feeling confused and depressed, anxious to get away and see new things.

And there was another problem, too, that I hoped a trip to Kim's parents' farm might solve.

From sitting with Kim on the sofa, from finding her long blond hairs in the sink and smelling her smell in every room, I was getting erections again after almost two whole years of peace.

* * *

When we dropped off my car at a Goodyear garage next to Maplewood Mall, Kim did not know it was part of my plan to take her to her family. I ordered a twelve-point safety check, a lube job, and an oil change. The mechanic said to come back in two hours.

The mall put us both in a lively mood, the way it was designed to do, and Kim said she was glad I had finally gotten her out of the house. There were waterfalls and carousels and rows of old-fashioned wooden park benches where you could sit and eat and watch the fun. The other shoppers seemed happy, too, though none quite so happy as Kim: she glowed. Her makeup and clothes and jewelry had been lost, left at her wrecked apartment—and yet, in the man's white dress shirt I had lent her and a pair of old jeans she'd been wearing for days, she carried herself like the queen of the mall. For our lunch, I bought slices of deep-dish pizza, and I gave Kim the change from my twenty for pocket money. It broke my heart and filled it, too, that the first coin she spent, she gave to charity: a quarter tossed high and girlishly into a Lions Club wishing well.

We went from store to store, visiting all three levels of the mall. Our first stop was a Rite Aid drugstore, where I bought a flashlight for the car, a five-pack of white cotton T-shirts for Kim, and a pair of nail clippers for me. The clippers were her idea, and she used them on me immediately. I stood in the mall aisle, gazing at the waterfall, as Kim trimmed and filed, pushing down my cuticles. I liked the feeling, the pain of proper hygiene, and when Kim was done, she showed me my hands as though they were something she'd made in an art class.

"There," she said. "Much better. Maybe now you won't hide them in your pockets."

"Do I do that?"

"You never take them out."

We wandered into Dayton's, a large department store. A well-dressed lady standing in the entrance offered to spritz some perfume on Kim's wrist. Kim unbuttoned her cuff, got sprayed, then held her arm up under my nose. I sensed an opportunity. I opened my wallet and paid for the perfume: twenty-eight dollars plus tax. Kim seemed a little shocked, but also pleased.

"You think it smells pretty?" she said.

"It's very pretty."

She sniffed her wrist. "You're sure you can afford it?"

I nodded; my mother's check had just arrived. "Someday, if you like," I said, "you can buy me some cologne. Right now, though, I want to buy you a few things. You've been through a lot—you deserve it."

I led Kim deeper into the store, into women's clothing. My intention was to build her confidence. I had learned from selling Sanipure that having new things makes people optimistic, at least for a day or two, and optimism was what I felt Kim needed. It would give her the courage to go to her family, ask for their support, and accept all the blessings I knew would follow.

Fingering fabrics, turning over price tags, we sorted through the outfits on the racks. I learned a lot about colors. Red, Kim informed me, goes best with black and white. Orange is a stimulant and blue calms people. She said she had learned these things in art school and from designing her cards. The cards again. That morning, in the kitchen trash can, I had discovered some scribbled-on napkins and asked Kim what they were. "Pathetic attempts at humor," she had said.

She spent an hour trying on clothes. I could see her

naked feet and ankles under the dressing-room door. Her ankles looked swollen, puffy. Her toenails were coated with chipped pink polish. Every few minutes, she opened the door, performed a little turn, and asked me what I thought. If I said I liked a certain dress, she would tug at the hem or fiddle with the buttons, shaking her head at the outfit's flaws. If I said I didn't like one, she would ask me why not and look hurt. The truth was she looked good in everything. What's more, her new perfume was starting to get to me.

In the end, I said yes to three outfits, despite an urge to buy them all. I didn't want Kim to know that, though; I wanted her to believe I had standards. I rejected one of the dresses she liked best and praised to the skies a V-neck top she said she wasn't sure about.

"I'm surprised," she said, fingering the collar. "I thought it might be too revealing for you."

Now that Kim had pointed it out to me, I saw that the cut was, in fact, rather low. Still, what's done is done.

After I paid for the clothes and for two pairs of shoes to go with them, Kim got a computer skin analysis. She said she didn't need one done ("I already know my complexion type: I'm fair"), but I was pleasing myself now, not her, and I wanted to see what she looked like all made up.

I held the shopping bags while Kim underwent the analysis and makeover. The lab-coated saleslady asked me not to watch—she said the results would gratify me most if they came as a surprise. I wandered down the aisle toward Home Appliances and was waylaid by the sight of my reflection in the smoked-glass door of a microwave oven. Something was wrong with my face. A wolfish look. A certain chilly glitter in my pupils. I had seen the look before, but not for ages; it frightened me, but I couldn't look away. I must have stared at myself for quite a while because, when I finally turned around, Kim was beside me, with a whole new smile.

"How am I?" she said.

I looked her up and down. The makeup technician had done an expert job, and Kim clearly knew it. Her eyes were wide and flirty. I looked at her newly highlighted cheekbones, the crescents of faint peach blush, the V-neck top. I felt my penis roll over in my boxers, the languid waking flop of a long-sedated creature. Suddenly, I was disgusted with myself.

"What's wrong?" Kim said. "You're pale."

"I'm fine."

"Aren't you going to tell me what you think?"

Kim misunderstood my silence. "You want me to take back the clothes?" she said. "They were too expensive, weren't they?"

I shook my head. "It's me. The problem's me. A person thinks he's made some progress, gained some self-control, and then he finds out . . ."

Kim reached out and touched my hand and said, "Don't be so hard on yourself. You're fine. You're great. You just have a little problem with your ding-a-ling."

I looked to the side, ashamed and angry, and focused on a row of washers and driers. I flashed on a dream I had had the night before. In the dream I was being baptized by Lucas, a total-immersion baptism in a lake. He cradled the back of my head in his palm and laid me down in the water. I opened my eyes and saw hundreds of fish. They darted and hovered, all different colors. I inhaled and found I could breathe underwater. When Lucas tried to raise me, I resisted, but he was too strong. He wrenched me back up. My face broke the surface and burned in the air.

I looked back at Kim, expecting to be punished. I had been leading her on, leading myself on, and lying about it. The clothes were for me, not her; soon they might not even fit. She should have slapped my face.

All she did was stand there, though, immobilized by her perfect appearance. The moment a woman feels truly beautiful, she wants to stay that way and never move.

It was up to me to take control. "I'm driving you home to your folks," I said. "We're not accomplishing anything here. I really think it's the wisest course."

Kim said, "Why is that?"

"You need your parents' advice, their backing. I promise you, once we've talked to them, you'll see what a blessing it is to have a family."

"Like you and your mother," she said.

"My mother and I are not a family. Once a soul is born again, God is its primary parent, not some person."

Kim knit her eyebrows. "You're strange. I used to think interesting-strange, but you're just strange. I mean it. Maybe you should see someone."

"See a professional?"

"Maybe it would help."

I sucked in my gut, preparing to be cruel. "That's your solution to everything," I said. "Have a doctor fix it."

Kim turned around and walked off. She zigzagged between the appliances, head down, almost bumping into other shoppers. I think we both knew that it was an experiment: she was leaving to see if I would follow; I was staying put to see if I could let her go.

Or maybe this was the end—I couldn't tell.

I watched as the clock on the microwave oven ticked

away ten minutes, then picked up the shopping bags and left the mall. I crossed the crowded parking lot to the Goodyear garage. I didn't expect Kim to be there, and she wasn't. That would have made things too easy on me, and I deserved a harder lesson. I had waited the whole insulting ten minutes to make Kim mad enough to give me one.

I cruised the crowded parking lot, making systematic passes up and down the rows. I thought I would find her eventually, but I hoped it would be at the point when I was desperate, about to give up. That way, finding Kim would be a gift. It would prove to me that she was free, that I missed her, and consequently I would have a choice: accept these facts or watch her leave again.

But that is not how it happened. I found Kim almost immediately, before I began to miss her, before I had to swear a single pledge. She was sitting on a pickup bumper, smoking, her hair a tangled mess. A pair of black mascara streaks ran down her cheeks to the sides of her mouth like the jaw-cracks on a ventriloquist's dummy.

She waved to me and I stopped the car. I thought about getting out and going to her but saw it would not be necessary: she was already coming to me.

Just when she could have had me, just when she could have put me in my place, Kim had given up.

She climbed in beside me, still crying. She took a long drag on her cigarette, then flicked it out the window. "I'm selfish," she said. "You're right. I'm ruining my body. Ruining my life. I think I'm so exceptional, so special—what a fucking joke. My mother had three kids. Three of us." She turned to me, holding her hand up: three fingers. "Weaver, you have to forgive me." Her face was pouty, like a little girl's. "You have to forgive what a selfish bitch I've been."

What I did next was wrong, perhaps sinful: I accepted an apology that wasn't even owed to me, or to any person. Accepted it as if I were God himself.

"I forgive you," I said.

Kim laid her head on my shoulder. I patted her hair and made a hushing sound. I wasn't sure how or why, but things had changed between us, and I sensed she would do what I asked of her now. She was begging me to lead. The man. The way it is supposed to be.

Eleven

I WOKE UP EARLY, PRAYED AND SHOWERED, SPENT FIFTEEN RO-
botic minutes lifting dumbbells, then packed some
clothes in a nylon overnight bag for the trip to North
Dakota.

I was planning on a two- or three-day visit, just long
enough to get Kim settled in and see that her parents
understood the challenges they and their daughter now
faced. Although Kim hadn't told me much about them
("What can I say? They're farmers"), I assumed that her
folks would take her news well. A grandchild—they
would have to take it well. But just in case there were
problems, I would be on hand to smooth things over. Then
I would come back alone to St. Paul and . . . I really hadn't
thought that far ahead. I knew I had some decisions to

make, about work, about church, about my life in general, but I was putting off thinking about them in order to give Kim my full attention. Once I knew she and her baby were safe, I would be free to think about myself.

Kim was still asleep as I filled my shaving kit with sample-size Sanipure toiletries. She had been up for most of the night, making noisy round trips to the bathroom. The pee just dribbled out of her, she said; she couldn't control her bladder. She woke me up to talk about it, sitting down beside me on the sofa and nervously picking lint balls off my blanket. I explained to her that frequent urination was common in pregnant women, and I sent her to bed with a medical guidebook written by a Christian gynecologist: *The Nine-Month Miracle*. For the rest of the night, whenever I turned over, I could smell the wet spot where she'd sat.

It smelled like garlic toast.

Oddly, I didn't mind it.

I finished packing at nine o'clock and stowed my bag in the trunk of the car. I went back upstairs to start a pot of coffee. Kim had on one of my purple Vikings T-shirts and was standing in the bedroom doorway, hugging a pillow against her chest.

"You need to come look at something," she said. "I don't know what it is. I'm scared."

I followed Kim into the bedroom and looked where she was pointing, at the bottom bedsheet.

Because I had read so many books on pregnancy, I knew right away that a drop or two of blood was nothing to be concerned about. I stripped the blanket off the bed to see if there was more blood. There wasn't—just two soiled dents from Kim's heels. On the bedside table I noticed a saucer heaped with cigarette butts; they upset me more than the blood did. Yesterday, coming back from the mall, Kim had pledged to quit smoking, and yet she must have held on to her pack. I wondered if all her vows were just as meaningless.

She clutched the pillow and nodded at the bed. "Is that what a miscarriage looks like?"

"I really wish you'd read that book I gave you. It's what they call spotting," I said. "It's normal."

"Hold me," said Kim. "I'm scared."

I stepped back. "You're fine. Let's get you packed."

"Weaver, please—I'm *scared*."

It is hard to do your duty when other people are neglecting theirs. Lucas assaulting Melissa. Kim blowing clouds of tar and nicotine into her baby's vulnerable new body. There for a moment, I wanted out. God would get along fine without me. There was liquor to sell at my mother's store; I could sell it, and I would inherit the store. I didn't have to hug anyone. I didn't have to save anyone. I pictured myself in my mother's black sedan, a middle-aged small-town vice lord with cruise control and tinted power windows, driving up to a bank.

Kim's child, however, was still alive, still growing, and that was something I could be proud of. I thought of the cluster of cells inside her womb curled up in fluid, tiny fingers. I dreamed about it almost every night. I imagined the child was a boy and that he would grow up strong and healthy, surrounded by a loving circle of relatives and friends. Of course, he would never know what I had done for him, but I would know, and that would be enough. Someday, we'd throw a football around, go fishing for walleyes. Big brother Weaver.

I gave Kim her hug and it seemed to reassure her. I felt

calmer, too. When we got on the road a couple hours later, I reminded Kim to buckle up, then set the tripometer back to zero.

The towns got smaller and farther apart as we neared the North Dakota border. Blue Harvestore silos, each with a painted American flag, were the heroes of the landscape. The fields were stunted and yellow from drought, and tractors with slow-moving-vehicle triangles crept along the shoulder of the interstate. The deep-treaded tires threw off clods of dirt. In the upper part of my windshield, I could see the signature white trails of plains-based fighter-bombers.

Kim dozed for the first two hours. Her body sagged in the net of her shoulder belt, her hands sliding over her belly whenever I sped up to pass another car. Between her pale, veiny legs, on the floor, was what was left of lunch: a crumpled family pack of barbecue-flavor potato chips, a Snickers-bar wrapper, some dry-roasted peanuts. I had tried to get Kim to eat a cheese sandwich, but sugar and salt were her instincts today, and it was no use fighting them. Between all the carnival food and the cigarettes, her baby was getting an early dose of lazy American living. I wondered if he would be born addicted or immune.

At Sauk Centre, Minnesota, I turned on a Christian radio station, the only static-free signal on the dial. The Reverend Armand Dale of "Positions" was fielding calls from across the Midwest. The problems his callers wanted solved—cancer, divorce, unemployment—were all beyond his powers, and he said so. Again and again, he recommended prayer, but his callers went on whining anyway. I put up with them at first, but pretty soon I was mumbling back, telling the callers to quit their griping and get on their knees like everybody else. Eventually, I got so frustrated I switched to a staticky country-music station.

Kim sat up. "I was listening to that."

"You shouldn't have been. It's pathetic. Reverend Dale should not indulge those people."

Kim yawned. "I need to pee again. How far to a rest stop?"

"I'm sorry, we just passed one."

Kim rubbed her eyes and laid her cheek against the vinyl headrest. She seemed to be sweating a lot; I heard a sticky peeling sound whenever she shifted around in the seat. After another catnap, she said, "Thank you, Weaver. Thank you for the ride. I realize I haven't thanked you yet for everything you're doing."

"It's nothing. Go back to sleep." I switched on my wipers to clear off a wasp.

"I mean it—you're very sweet. My life got pretty screwed up back there. My values. Everything I was taught growing up went right out the window." She shook her head. "I guess the city can maybe do that to you. Kind of warp your perspective."

"Not just the city," I said. "The world."

Kim said, "The city especially. Before I moved down to St. Paul I was good. I didn't even let my boyfriends kiss me. Not with their tongues, I mean. Not French. Those farmboys are filthy, you can't imagine. Cruddy fingernails, always chewing snuff. They don't even wash their hair before school, just slick it down with motor oil or something. But then, in St. Paul, I lost my fear of germs. The men seemed so much cleaner there, so much better groomed. They drove me wild."

"Our souls have different ignition keys," I said, quoting

one of Pastor Spannring's favorite automotive metaphors.

"With me it was expensive socks," said Kim. "North Dakota guys have awful socks. They wear them all day doing chores, then turn them inside out for dates." She picked up a Coke can and took a sip that must have been warm and flat, then said, "Has anyone ever told you you're cute? You look like that movie actor, what's his name."

"I hope I don't resemble any actor. I don't see how I could."

"You do, though. That guy in those teenage movies. He must be almost thirty, but he plays eighteen-year-olds. Guys with dimples never seem to age."

"I don't have dimples."

"Sure you do."

"Well, I don't look eighteen."

"It's more like sixteen."

Kim had struck a sore spot; I turned the radio back on to discourage further conversation. The fact was I had never looked my age, and I was sick of it. Well into my teens, my mother the businesswoman, always alert to financial opportunities, had capitalized on my immature appearance in the form of child-priced movie tickets, kiddie dinner specials, cut-rate plane fares, and countless other juvenile discounts. Of course, once on board the plane or sitting in the restaurant, I was expected to grow up instantly and not only act my true age but much older. I had to spread a napkin on my lap, sip not slurp my drink, and nod politely at my mother's stories of firing her latest accountant or completing a storewide inventory. So she could save fifty cents or a dollar, I was routinely forced to transform myself from under twelve to at least twenty-one in less than a couple of minutes. Craziest was the week I turned fourteen, when my mother and I visited an art museum. She had sprained an ankle a few days before and was using a metal cane to get around. She gave me a five-dollar bill and sent me to the ticket booth with instructions to buy a child's pass for myself and a senior citizen's for her. She slumped on the cane with her back turned as I conducted the fraudulent transaction. When I turned around with the passes, though, I saw a strange old woman, all stooped over, and forgot that my mother was acting. She seemed too ancient to have given birth to me; I wondered if I'd been kidnapped. Whisked away. Perhaps she had lived in some castle in the forest, alone with her caldron and her book of spells, and I had skipped past her window one day. . . .

I was stuck in this sinkhole of a memory when a highway-patrol car's flashing blue lights swept across the rearview. I eased my foot off the gas. The car shot past. I estimated its speed at over ninety.

Kim crossed her legs and adjusted the lap of her new yellow sundress. I sensed she was making a brave attempt to keep her mind off her bladder. "Tell me about your last girlfriend," she said. "What was she like? Did you love her?"

"I just saw a sign for the rest stop. Thirty-three more miles, if you can make it."

"Can't you talk about her?"

I could, in fact, but I didn't see the point. Her name was Tina, and yes, I'd thought I loved her. She was one of those sweet-faced, heavy-drinking women who always have two boyfriends at a time: one to beat them up, and one to show their bruises to. I was the one who kissed the bruises, the one who gave her sympathy. The one who always gets dumped for the other one.

This was how I compressed it for Kim: "My last girl-friend wasn't a girlfriend. She wasn't anything."

I expected Kim to press me for details; instead, she began to talk about herself. "I guess the only guy I ever loved was Leo Alexander. He was the one who got me doing cards. He's a terrific designer. He's an artist."

In a way that had always annoyed me, she pronounced the word *artist* as though it meant *saint*. My mother the businesswoman did it, too.

"I never found Leo attractive," said Kim, "but I loved him because he loved me. He gave me self-confidence. Really built me up. I didn't have a goal before I met him. My only goal was leaving North Dakota."

"What happened?" I said. "Did he drop you?" Kim had drawn me into silly girl-talk, but at least it passed the time. I wished I could drive as fast as the police car—we would have been there by now.

Kim said, "We drifted apart, we just lost touch. I think he was probably queer. A gay. I can really pick 'em, huh? I mean, now I meet you and you're celibate or something."

"Not celibate. Waiting for marriage. There's an important difference."

Kim laughed. "You'll get married when I get married: never. Except, with you, it'll be by choice. With me, it'll be . . . I just can't picture it. Not with a North Dakota guy, at least."

"Is it hard to be going back?"

"Not really," said Kim. "I guess I had my fun."

Our conversation petered out. I felt sleepy myself now. I was about to ask Kim for the Coke when I topped a low hill and saw the state-patrol car parked up ahead on the shoulder.

Then I saw the wreck.

There was only one car, a black, late-model Jeep. It lay on its side in the passing lane surrounded by a sleet of broken glass and various personal items, clothes and things, that must have flown out the windows when it rolled. The trail of wreckage led back across the median, meaning the Jeep must have tumbled several times and for quite a distance.

Immediately, I thought, *No survivors.* I stopped the car maybe fifty feet back because there was so much debris on the road; I was afraid of puncturing a tire. I put my hand on Kim's knee and looked at her. Her face was dead pale, but her eyes were wide open. Her lips were sucked back tight against her teeth.

"You stay here," I said.

I set the parking brake and got out.

Human ribs, I learned that day, are whiter than you'd think. They shine. So do other body parts that are never exposed to air. The expression *bright pink lungs* is not poetic but straight-on description. And bile, if that's what I saw, is truly green. For things that God created to stay hidden, internal organs are strangely showy.

The patrolman knelt in a puddle of coolant facing the vehicle's upturned roof. I stood a few yards back from him, wondering if I should offer assistance. He seemed unaware of my presence. What he appeared to be trying to do was determine some fact concerning the body, which lay partway under the side of the Jeep. The patrolman wore white latex gloves and a face mask held on by a rubber band. He poked at the body with an index finger, an oddly cautious jabbing motion a child might use to wake a sleeping pet. He picked up a scrap of what looked like bloody fabric, examined it at arm's length, then put it back down on the ground. He kept the hand well away from him as he slowly stood.

He turned around and saw me standing there. I expected him to yell at me, but all he said was, "You witness it?" His words were slightly muffled by the face mask.

"No," I said, "I just drove up."

"Must have been speeding and lost control. It's perfect road conditions." He nodded at me to move back and said, "Can't be too careful out here—there's a breeze. AIDS only takes a microscopic droplet."

The patrolman and I started back toward our cars. He reached his car first; I watched him open the trunk. He took out a small cardboard box with an indistinguishable symbol on the side. He lifted the box lid and peeled off his gloves, then dropped them inside, followed by his mask. He closed the box and put it in the trunk.

Back inside my car, I sat with my hand on the shift knob, thinking. Kim was sniffling, dabbing at her eyes, and she did not interrupt me. When I felt ready to drive again, I started the car and went off the pavement, into a field, to get around the wreck.

We didn't use the rest stop. A couple of miles farther down the road, Kim said she couldn't hold it anymore and made me pull over. She squatted behind her open door, holding on to the armrest and casting shy backward glances as her stream jetted noisily onto the gravel.

Once we were back on our way and Kim had recomposed herself, she said, "So what was the story there? What happened? I couldn't see a thing."

"The driver fell out and got crushed." My head was still in a daze. I touched my temple.

"Only one body?"

"I don't know. I think so."

Kim said, "Was it difficult to look at?"

I decided it must have been and nodded.

"A man or a woman?" Kim said.

I paused for a moment to think about that, and Kim repeated the question. She seemed to believe the answer mattered. Then it came to me: what the patrolman's jabbing and poking must have been about.

He was trying to learn the sex of the victim, and I was almost sure he'd failed. We all look the same on the inside, especially after a major trauma. Human blood is human blood.

Nevertheless, I answered Kim's question, and in a manner I still don't understand. Certain lies are so unnecessary you wonder why you bother to tell them, except that you think they will make life more interesting.

"It was a man. A young man," I said. "My age. I had the exact same wreck last winter, in that exact kind of car. I nearly died. Only thing that saved me was my seat belt."

I looked to the side to check Kim's reaction, but she had turned away from me, toward her rolled-down window, and all I could see was the sweat stain on the back of her new yellow dress.

Twelve

WE STOOD ON THE PORCH IN THE DARK AND KNOCKED AND knocked. Above the front door, a fluorescent insect trap was attracting the largest moths I'd ever seen. They fluttered against the electrified wires and perished in hectic bursts of purple sparks. The dust of their bodies drifted down and settled dandrufflike on our shoulders.

"You didn't call ahead?" I said. I had asked Kim last night to call ahead.

"I think you should maybe know something, Weaver. My folks and I don't get along too well. It's nothing serious, just . . . differences. Also, they call me Agnes, not Kim."

I waited, hands on hips, for an explanation.

Kim brushed a spot of bug dust off her dress. "Agnes is my first name, Kim's my middle. Naming a little girl Agnes these days is child abuse, in my opinion. I switched things around when I ran away."

I looked to the side; I felt angry, tricked. Already, the visit was getting complicated. Down the dirt road that led to the farm, in a neighbor's yard, a boy was sweeping a flashlight beam back and forth across the lawn—shining for night crawlers, maybe, or searching for something lost in the grass.

"To me, I was going to art school," said Kim. "To Dixie, my mom, I was running away. Like I said: we're different."

I walked toward the end of the porch, feeling a need for a moment alone after the shoulder-to-shoulder car trip. My foot touched something hard, and I looked down. A plastic milk crate lined with flannel rags sheltered a litter of sleeping kittens. Kim came up and knelt down and stroked their little cowlicked heads. The kitten she picked up was starvation-thin and its eyes were stuck shut—infected, it looked like. She picked up another and it was the same.

"I think those need a vet," I said.

Kim said, "Vets are for livestock, not pets," and her voice had a sudden pioneer sternness. She licked a finger and dabbed the kitten's eyes clean. Then she held the poor animal out to me. I kept my hands at my sides and wouldn't take it, certain it had parasites. Kim said, "You silly," and scratched the kitten's ears until it made a sound. It was a side of her I'd never seen. Clearly, she was at home in the world of other creatures, while I had never even owned a pet. Animals frightened me. Their nakedness. The way you could always see their anuses.

"Why's it so puny?" I said. "Is it sick?"

"Possibly. Or else it's fine. That's the thing with farm cats: either they die as kittens or they never die." Kim cupped the runt against her shoulder and kissed the tips of its ears, then put it down. She picked up another and did the same with it: wipe, cuddle, kiss. Then she scooped up the whole bunch of them and nuzzled them all at once, rubbing her chin in the fur. She held out a kitten, and this time I took it.

I just couldn't resist the picture we made.

For a Swedish family's farmhouse, there wasn't much food in the kitchen—but then I had certain ideas about farmhouses. Samplers, for example: I expected them. GOD BLESS OUR HOME and so on. Also, I expected crockery. Big brown jars marked FLOUR, HONEY, SUGAR. But this kitchen wasn't like that; it was modern. Modern in the way that kitchens were before people started decorating them to fit their notions of farmhouse kitchens. This place was chilly, unwelcoming, bare, with scuffed yellow tile, Formica counters, and off-brand TV dinners in the fridge.

Kim put two Salisbury steaks in the oven and went upstairs to take a shower. I sat down at the white dinette and leafed through a magazine, *Dairyman Today*. The table had so many magazines on it and so much other junk—pliers, scissors, balls of twine—that I wondered if Kim's folks ate here anymore. It was important to me that they should. I wanted them to be typical Americans. Solid citizens. Suitable grandparents.

I sat at the table with a glass of water and browsed through a color photo-spread on Holsteins. The pictures seemed faded—I checked the cover date: August 1980. The rest of the magazines were just as old. I didn't know what to make of this. Perhaps the dairy industry hadn't

progressed much in the last twelve years. That, or the
Lindgrens hadn't progressed much.

I heard the shower splash on upstairs and decided that
this was my chance to have an unsupervised look around
the house. Depending on Kim's folks' attitude toward
me—if they ever came home, that was—I might have to
get a motel room tonight. And after Kim told them her
news, there might be no reason for me to come back here.
In the meantime, I felt an obligation to conduct a background check. For all I knew, and for all Kim had told
me, her parents might be drunks.

I started in the living room, and immediately I was
encouraged. The television, an old-fashioned console
with a built-in record player, was situated in such a
way—off by itself in a corner—that I guessed it was seldom used. The room's centerpiece was a book-laden coffee table, another good sign: Kim's parents were readers.
The pictures on the paneled walls also met with my ap-
proval. Unlike the abstract African art in my mother's
house (she collected the work of a Rwandan painter who
specialized in mysterious stick figures trapped inside
large, perfect rectangles), the Lindgrens' pictures were all
familiar scenes: a mountain at sunset, a covered bridge,
some cowboys boiling coffee on a campfire. The pictures
made the room feel safe, and I wished that I had grown
up with them in my house. My mother's idea of art, so
far as I had ever understood it, was that it should make
you nervous all the time.

Off to my right, I noticed a side room, door half-open,
light turned out. I entered it on tiptoes, flipped the wall
switch. The wall in front of me boasted a row of oval brass
plaques certifying Mr. Charles Lindgren as a Grade A dairy
farmer. The plaques' engraved dates were all from the

1970s. On the desk beneath the plaques stood a home computer, one of the earliest IBM PCs, its keyboard and screen silted over with dust. I sensed the machine had never been used, a failed attempt at modernization, and I found evidence for this conclusion in the form of a boxed accounting program standing next to the monitor, its original plastic wrapper intact. The only other object on the desk was a framed snapshot of a man in dirty overalls putting his arm around a cow's neck and grinning with pride of ownership. Written above the cow's head were the words *Chuck's top yielder!* I don't know why, but that exclamation point made my eyes mist over.

I returned to the living room and sat down on the couch, my curiosity satisfied. I picked up one of the books from the coffee table: a travel guide to Mexico. Beneath it I saw a travel guide to Florida. I soon discovered that all the books were travel guides. Hawaii, the Caribbean, Spain, Australia. I wondered what it meant.

I was trying to stack the books back the way they had been when I saw the headlights in the window.

He must have been thirty, perhaps thirty-five, but he dressed like a drag-strip teenager. His tight black sleeveless T-shirt advertised the rock band Anthrax and hung down just short of his thin, slitted navel. His jeans were also black, with too much room in the seat and hips. I didn't have to ask him his name because it was soldered in inch-high brass letters to his shieldlike belt buckle: Ricky.

He stood in the doorway, frowning, his fleshless arms hanging straight at his sides, anchored by six-packs of bottled beer. "And who are you?" he said.

"I'm Weaver. Nice to meet you. I'm a friend of Kim's."

He plunked down the six-packs on the kitchen counter and took out two bottles but didn't open them. "Who's Kim?" he said.

I remembered: "Agnes."

Ricky said, "Good for her. She finally changed it. Wait until Mom finds out about *that*." He twisted the caps off two bottles and held one out to me.

"No, thank you," I said. "I'm not drinking these days."

Ricky said, "Tough beans. I opened these," and went to the kitchen table, apparently expecting me to join him. When I sat down, he handed me a bottle, and foam ran out the neck and down the sides.

"That's ale," he said. "From England. The American shit I can't taste. Last year when I worked at the methanol plant I breathed in lots of chemicals and burned off my taste buds." He stuck out his tongue. "See—no taste buds."

I made a show of looking.

"Your sister is in the shower," I said. "She should be down in a minute."

"How's the ale?"

Out of politeness and some intimidation, I took the tiniest sip. "It's very rich."

"Good," said Ricky. "Me, I just can't taste it." He opened a copy of *Dairyman Today* and read for a while in silence, moving his thin, bluish lips. Alarmingly intense expressions played across his face. He pushed his long, greasy hair behind his ears and said, "You read this yet? This article on price supports?"

"No, I didn't get to it." My words sounded odd to me, muffled. I realized I had been swallowing my ale.

"Well, get to it," said Ricky. "It's enlightening. Know what I mean by 'enlightening'? Depressing. Price supports are welfare, classic welfare. I'd get you to sign my petition about them, but I can see that you're not from this state. The party I'm forming is just for North Dakotans."

"What is your party called?"

"It *will* be called Dakota First, once I pull my head out and get some signatures. Basically, it's a protest party. We're powerless, we know it, and we don't give a fuck. But that's our secret. Losers *über alles.*"

Caught off guard by the vehemence of Ricky's manifesto, I steadied myself by drinking more ale. The sound of Kim's shower had not let up. I was on my own down here.

My next thought was spoken by Ricky himself: "I sure wish Chuck and Dixie would get back." He lifted his arm and turned his head and gave his armpit an ugly canine sniff. "Boy, do I need some laundry done!"

"When do you expect them in?" I said.

Ricky reached into the six-pack on the table, opened two more bottles, gave me one, then returned my empty to the pack. "I'm a big recycler," he said. "It's going to pay in the long run, you just watch. If you believe in the long run, I mean. Some people don't. The apocalyptics."

I nodded—this was a subject I could talk about: "I know a few of those." Indeed, I knew more than a few. Half the Bryce Street Church of God was betting on Armageddon before the year 2000. The optimists gave us a year or two more.

Ricky sniffed his shirt again. "I reek."

"When are your folks expected?" I repeated.

"That depends. If they're losing, tomorrow, or maybe the next day. If they're on a hot streak, could be anytime, depending on what the flights are out of Vegas."

Gamblers.

The Lindgrens were gamblers.

I drank some ale and said, "I hope they get back soon. I also hope they win."

"They won't," said Ricky. "That Caesars Palace has got Chuck and Dixie exactly where it wants them. Chuck's dairy co-op gets some kind of deal there, everything half-price. They ought to—they blow enough money in the joint. Not that it's their dough to blow. It's taxes: yours and mine. The agri-dole. Between the set-aside, price supports, and the goddamn drought-disaster loans, the Rough Rider State is fucking Harlem North now."

"I'm sorry to hear that," I said.

Ricky chewed his thumbnail, brooding. "Myself, I'd rather live in New York Harlem. Better music there. North Dakotans don't believe in music, don't believe in sound of any kind. The odd burp, the random beer fart, that's about it up here on the prairie. Most nights, you can hear the neighbors' taps drip."

I listened: Kim's shower had stopped. I hoped she was coming down to rescue me. I had finished my second bottle of ale, and I needed a reason to stop before my third. Ricky scared me, made me want to drink. Or maybe it was the bubble that scared me—the way I could feel it sealing around me, a perfect globe of silence. But it was already too late: I watched my hand go reaching for the six-pack and extract another chilly bottle. I told myself not to panic: the Lord, while he was on earth, drank, too. In moderation, I'd always assumed, and only red wine, but how did I know?

I didn't know a thing.

Ricky lit a cigarette and said, "What's she doing here, anyway? She broke? I warned her she'd go broke down there."

I gave a strange answer. A bubble answer. An answer for when you feel you can't be heard and might as well speak your actual thoughts. "Kim was lost. I saved her."

Ricky grinned. "So you're her boy now?"

"Mmm."

"You know about all the other ones?"

"Mmm."

Ricky blew a smoke ring that hung intact between us for the longest time. "So what was she lost in?" he said. "Just shit? Just the same old shit? Or what?"

Even inside the thickening bubble, I knew that Kim's secret was not mine to tell. Ricky could hear me—I had to assume that. I watched him reach into the pocket of his jeans and take out a black plastic jar, a film canister. He thumbed off the lid, leaned forward, and held out the canister under my nose.

"Get a whiff," he said. "It's killer. I grow it myself from Jamaican seeds."

The marijuana smell—dusty, clinging, sweet—might as well have been filling the universe.

After a moment of awful struggle that seemed to be occurring someplace else, somewhere up high and at the edge of things, I summoned the strength to turn my nose away.

"I'm sorry," I said. "I quit smoking. I'm a Christian."

I waited to see if the word alone would shield me, or if I would have to stand up and leave the house.

"No problem," said Ricky. "Who isn't? I'm one, too." He closed the canister, slipped it in his pocket. "Up here, it's either grow weed or go on food stamps. I'm not especially proud of it myself."

The victory seemed too easy. I set down my ale, and that was easy, too. I looked at Ricky, facing down the

117

Tempter, but he was not the Tempter anymore, just a very strange young man with deep, mysterious grievances.

"Relax," he said. "Enjoy your ale. You must be tired from driving." He tipped back his head and hollered, "Agnes!"

"What?"

Kim's voice seemed to come from the overhead light. I looked up and saw a metal grate. She was right on top of us.

"What are you doing?" Ricky said.

"Cleaning up my bedroom. What's it to you?"

Ricky looked at me, cracked a smile. Then, to the ceiling again: "You mean spying. Listening in on your Christian boyfriend and motorhead brother. Gettin' all the dope."

Kim said, "Give it a rest. I just got here."

"At least you gave it a go down there," said Ricky. "Well, welcome home to the Failure State. It's always a treat to see our native youth come limping back with empty gas tanks."

I had to get outside. I rose from the table on foam-rubber legs and opened the door and went out to the porch. Kim and Ricky's banter just grew louder—I plastered my hands on my ears to shut it out. The air was cool, with a breeze that smelled of wheat. I took a few breaths and started feeling better. I sat on a step and looked up at the stars, which seemed brighter and sharper than in the Twin Cities. Here, you could see why they called them the heavens, and why they called the moon a lunar body.

I wanted to be a spirit, up there with them, traveling outward at unheard-of speeds.

Thirteen

THE DOWNSTAIRS GUEST ROOM RICKY PUT ME IN WAS A NIGHT-time echo chamber. In the wall behind my pillow, enterprising mice improved their dwellings. Somewhere off to my left, Ricky hawked and coughed and spat, shifting the heavy cargo of his lungs. Above me, Kim's tippy-toe trips to the bathroom climaxed in overwhelming flushes that stormed in the pipes for minutes afterward. I lay on my back on top of the bedspread and tried to ignore the commotion. When I finally felt myself falling asleep, a songbird on a branch outside my window went off like an alarm clock. It was Sunday morning.

I dragged my aching head and heavy limbs to the kitchen table and sat there for a while amid the empty ale bottles, hoping a thought would come to me, any thought. I needed a thought for the day. A beginning.

A friend in need is a friend indeed.

He will not fail thee, nor forsake thee.

For all its faults, the United States remains the greatest country in the world.

Do your best.

I went with *Do your best.*

As the first one out of bed, I took it upon myself to fix breakfast. I scrambled a half dozen eggs, ignoring the carton's long-passed expiration date, and mixed up a pitcher of orange Tang. I would have made toast, but the loaf in the breadbox was tufted with greenish mold.

I covered the pan of eggs with foil and put it in the oven to keep warm. Then I had an idea. I found a plate, a glass, a fork, and a tin TV tray embossed with pictures of John Deere tractors. The glass was a giveaway item, too; it bore the logo of AgBan Herbicides. I hunted around for a daintier glass, but the best I could do was a Texaco tumbler. Chuck and Dixie Lindgren, I decided, were the thriftiest gamblers ever to hit Vegas.

I went upstairs and down a hall to where I guessed Kim's bedroom was. My hands were full with the breakfast tray, so I nudged the door with my knee—gently, because I wanted to surprise her.

At first, I thought I had the wrong room. I didn't see a bed, just a chest-high pyramid of dusty yard-sale clutter. The bottom layer was made up of toys. There were board games, from Monopoly to Clue, in battered cardboard boxes. There were cap pistols, jump ropes, a kinked and rusty Slinky, and several G.I. Joe and Barbie dolls locked in obscene, akimbo embraces. The next layer up was children's winter clothes: pink puffball mittens, snowboots, stocking caps. There were four pairs of skates—two figure, two hockey—and perhaps a dozen volumes, of the *World Book Encyclopedia*, lying facedown and broken-spined. The rest of the pile was shoes.

Tap shoes, gym shoes, work boots, moccasins—the Lindgren Memorial Footwear Museum.

I heard Kim's voice from somewhere in the room: "Weaver, is that you?"

I stepped to the side and looked around the junk heap. Kim lay in bed in a pink flannel nightgown printed with faded Disney cartoons. The nightgown might have fit her as a twelve-year-old, but now it barely reached her thighs. Her pose on the bed seemed both innocent and calculated—the sleepy, curled-up disarray of a thumb-sucking seductress. She rolled on her side and faced me. "Come here."

"I thought you might like some breakfast," I said, nodding at the plate of cooling eggs.

"Thanks. I'll eat it later. Come here and feel my stomach."

I set the tray on a table by the bed, then sat on the edge of the mattress and said, "Is something wrong again? More spotting?"

"I'm fine." Kim drew up her nightie and took my hand and laid it on her skin, an inch or two lower than I thought decent. "Don't be squeamish," she said. "Just feel."

I felt.

Kim moved my hand down until it touched a soft place.

"What are you doing?" I said. "You're doing something."

"There," she said. "That's me. You're touching me now." She took away her hand and left mine lying there. "I had the sweetest dream of us. We were out on a boat, a lifeboat, at night, waving at a giant lit-up cruise ship. Silver fish were jumping all around us, landing in our laps. You were trying to row us toward an island, but it was too windy. Our hair was blowing everywhere. I had a flare gun and I shot it off. There was a beautiful burst of purple sparks, like a huge umbrella, but no one could see it but us. The ship was gone."

I nodded, feeling dizzy.

I was dizzy because I could not control the temperature.

My hand was warm and my face was hot and the breakfast was getting cold.

Things stayed that way until Kim rolled over and moved my hand off her belly. "You run along downstairs," she said. She tucked her legs up tight against her body and drew down the nightie over her knees. "I want to go back to my dream now. See if we ever reach that island."

I watched her close her eyes.

After breakfast, Ricky asked me to go with him to church—a Nazarene congregation down in Fargo—but once we were on the road in his van, we agreed that we weren't in the mood for formal services. Instead, we decided to worship via satellite, with the Mormon Tabernacle Choir. Ricky had quite a car stereo, with multiple hidden speakers and an equalizer. He dialed the volume knob all the way up, and a sudden blast of "Rock of Ages" nearly boosted me out of my seat.

Riding along, I could see that the van was more than transportation—it was Ricky's home. The walls were upholstered from floor to ceiling in a purple crushed velour that reminded me of the linings used in caskets. Behind Ricky's seat was a compact stove-refrigerator stocked, no doubt, with English ale. The rest of the cabin was taken up by a double mattress and box springs heaped with dirty laundry. A sour morning-after odor permeated everything.

Ricky muted the music and said, "Either we can go back home, or we can run some errands. Your choice." He spoke the word *home* in a tone of defeat and *errands* as if it meant *adventures*.

I pictured Kim in her Minnie Mouse nightie asleep beside the mountain of old toys. I thought about what had just happened between us, sitting on her bed. I wondered what her dream of us had meant and decided I could use a few free hours before I went back to all that.

"Some errands," I said, and Ricky said, "You got it."

He crushed the gas pedal flat to the floor and cranked up the Mormon hymns to a level I hadn't expected to hear till after death.

By the time we reached Kim and Ricky's sister Bev's house, we had polished off an ale or two (a headache cure, I told myself) and were singing along with the choir. Ricky parked the van in Bev's front yard, a square of grassless, tramped-down dirt whose only decoration was an imitation-marble birdbath filled with urinous rainwater. The house was a one-story rambler set in a large, graded field marred by a number of dead-end driveways—the remains of a subdivision, it looked like, that had not quite taken off. As we climbed down from the van, Ricky explained that Bev and her kids were staying in Alaska for the summer, visiting her oil-driller husband, and that's why the yard was in such poor condition.

"Actually, Bev's pretty house-proud," he said. "I don't know where she got it. Not from Dixie."

Following Ricky's example, I left my ale bottle out on

the porch and took off my shoes in the mudroom. The house was small and tidy. Tinted antique photographs and assembly-line prints of wildlife lined the walls. In every room I saw a box of Kleenex, its topmost tissue thoughtfully puffed out. Ricky seemed proud to be showing me around, as if his sister's well-kept home reflected honor on the family name. Several times he praised Bev's knack for making the most of limited space. He talked about the bunk beds in the kids' room as if she had invented the concept.

I asked him if Kim and Bev were close. My thought was that Kim had a lot to learn from her sister's domestic ways.

Ricky said, "They used to get along—until they started school. Then they fought like hell. It's hard for twins."

"Kim has a twin?" I said. It hurt me that there was so much she hadn't told me. I thought I had done all I could to earn her trust.

Ricky showed me a photograph on top of the piano. Bev shared all Kim's features, it was true, except for the long blond hair, which Bev had cut short and dyed an orange color I associated with dead comediennes. Also, Bev appeared older than Kim. Her arms hung down so limply at her sides it looked as if she were waiting for the day when they would just drop off. Her eye sockets were truly sockets.

"Twins are nuts," said Ricky. "They're insane. Bev gets white shoes, Agnes needs a black pair. Bev starts dating jocks, Agnes sets her sights on the debate team. Bev gets married, Agnes hits the road."

"That's when she left?" I said. "When Bev got married?" Things were becoming clearer now.

Ricky said, "Day of the wedding," and patted the top

of the wide-screen TV next to the piano. "Come on, let's get to work. I need your help to lift this."

We crouched beside the cabinet and heaved. I walked backward and Ricky gave directions. Once we had loaded the set in his van, I asked him what we were doing.

He answered me with a long, sad story. Bev and her husband, Ricky said, were bankrupt. They had lost their family savings on a whole-grain-muffin scheme. For twenty thousand dollars, they had purchased the plans for a franchise shop called Dough Dough Land, as well as Fargo-wide rights to the name, a baking oven, and several secret recipes. Ricky said the reps from Dough Dough Land had conned Bev's husband into believing that whole-grain muffins were overtaking doughnuts as the American breakfast snack of choice, but unfortunately for him and Bev, said Ricky, the muffin trend just never made it out here. The shop, in a strip mall next to the freeway, had closed its doors exactly four weeks after its festive grand opening.

The whole sorry episode, Ricky said, was typical of life in North Dakota: "Back East or out West, a craze starts. Either it's something we would never think of or else it's a thing we had in the past and out-of-staters talked us into stopping—using wood-burning stoves, for example. Whatever it is, we see it on TV, and everyone gets all excited: buys a muffin shop, gets to building stoves. Then, when we're ready to make our millions, we turn on the damned TV again and see how the whole idea is all pooped out. Take that oat-bran thing. You know how many farmers in this state switched from hay to oats that year?"

Ricky's face was red and blotchy as he gave the moral:

"Every time a North Dakotan looks beyond these borders, he gets nailed."

I said I understood his theories, but what did they have to do with taking Bev's TV set?

"Simple debt reduction," Ricky said. "Between the insurance claim for Bev and Mike and what I can get when I sell these items, everybody wins. Otherwise, it's food stamps all the way."

"Insurance fraud is a felony," I said. "You can go to jail."

Ricky said, "What's fraud about it? It's just another way of pawning stuff—items they shouldn't have bought in the first place. Bev and Mike approve, believe me. Last year, when I cashed in their air conditioner, their son got the pair of braces he needed."

I thought about this for a while then said, "You told me you grew marijuana for a living."

"I do, but it's a loser. My quality's fine, but my salesmanship sucks. I get around people who want to buy dope, and all I can think of is how they can't afford it, so I end up smoking it myself."

I knew what Ricky meant—it had been the same with me and Sanipure. I'd ring a doorbell, hear a baby cry, and the next thing I knew, I'd be back in my car, shoving my sample kit under the seat.

"So," said Ricky, "you going to turn me in?"

I looked at the ground and shook my head.

Ricky said, "You're okay. You're all right," and cuffed me on the arm. "We losers have to go easy on each other."

We went back into the house and started dismantling Bev's stereo.

* * *

We drove a few miles down the highway to a farm. The farmer wore a greasy khaki workshirt whose left sleeve was folded and pinned at the shoulder. He met us in the driveway with a dolly. I waited in the van as Ricky unloaded the stolen electronics and haggled with the one-armed farmer. I saw a few bills being passed and then a handshake. When Ricky got back in the van, I asked him if we should help the farmer push the dolly into his barn.

Ricky said, "We should, but he won't let us. Karl's the proudest man I know. He could have sued Ford Tractors when he lost that arm and never had to work again—instead, he started a sideline business. I admire the man."

The sun was high in the van's dusty windshield as we drove along, headed off on another errand. I opened two ales and handed one to Ricky. I needed a drink to ease my conscience. What bothered me was not what we had done, but how little what we had done was bothering me. It might have been due to lack of sleep or to all the sunshine on my face, but to me, Ricky's pawning seemed like nothing worse than what was required to get by in this sad place. I thought of the monthly check from my mother—liquor money, every dime—and how it had paid my rent these last few years and had even gone into the church collection plate.

Who was I to judge anyone?

The errand, our last of the day, was to check on the progress of Ricky's pot plantation. We turned off the paved road onto a dirt road, proceeded straight for a mile or two, then parked next to a cornfield. Ricky led me between the head-high rows to a weedy riverbank. The tea-colored water was slow and shallow, and in it I could see the squirming backs of feeding carp and suckers.

Ricky said, "It's gone. I should have known." He dropped to one knee and said, "See these stalks? These were eight feet high, I swear. That deputy took them all for himself."

"How did he know where they were?"

"I trusted him—we used to play high-school football together. He told me he wanted a joint for a party, but couldn't go into the bars to buy it or he'd lose his job."

"I'm sorry."

Ricky made a disgusted face. "I'm glad to get free of it: farming's for morons. I don't care what you grow, it's one long heartbreak."

Ricky sat down on the creek bank and took off his shoes and stretched his legs and dipped his feet in the water. I joined him. Minnows swam up and nibbled our toes, a feeling halfway between ticklish and unsanitary.

After a silence, Ricky said, "I told you last night I'm a Christian. Maybe you doubted me, though."

I said nothing.

"Well, I am," he said. "And you know why?"

I shook my head.

"Because I love the stories. David and Goliath, that's my favorite. The crash of the Tower of Babel—that one, too. Also, when Jesus trashes the temple because of all the money changers. Myself, I like the action in religion." He slipped a hand inside his denim jacket and produced a small stone pipe already packed with marijuana. "What about yourself?" he said.

"I like the stories, too." I watched him light the pipe.

"Why else?"

"I don't know. It's personal. Something to do with my mother, I suppose. I just knew there had to be something in the universe at least as big as her."

Ricky inhaled with his eyes closed, seeming to understand. I imagined I could see inside his brain. The cells would glow for a moment, then wither. Obviously, he thought the glow was worth it.

Perhaps it was.

He blew out smoke and said, "One other question." His voice was trembly, higher than before. "If Agnes is really your sweetheart, then how come you didn't sneak up and sleep with her? I wasn't standing guard or anything."

I picked up a stone and closed my palm around it. "That's kind of personal, too."

"Come on," he said.

I wondered if I could trust him. Maybe so. Ricky set very low standards for himself, but at least he managed to keep them.

"Kim's not really my sweetheart," I said.

"Crap. My sister likes you fine."

I looked at his slitty red eyes. "How do you know?"

"Happy fat. She's put on happy fat." He offered the pipe; I waved it off. "If it's just that you're shy with girls," he said, "I'll help you. Not that I'm Don Casanova myself, just that I know my sister Agnes."

"It's complicated."

"Sure it is."

"It involves my beliefs," I said. "And circumstances."

Ricky nodded, then started to giggle. His giggling seemed uncontrollable. He covered his mouth with the back of his hand and a trickle of spit ran out between the fingers. He wiped the hand on his shirt and said, "Just about covers everything, huh? *Beliefs and circumstances!* Let's write that one down. Let's print a T-shirt."

I made a decision then: I took the pipe from Ricky's hand and held it to my lips. I wanted to be with him in his bubble and see what was making him laugh so hard, and if it would make me laugh, too. He touched the flame of his lighter to the bowl and I took a powerful, scorching drag.

We had spent a whole Sunday together, two losers, and suddenly I was just so tired of all the separation.

Fourteen

Kim said, "They're home. They won. A lot. They say they want to treat us all to dinner." She had on one of the dresses I'd bought her, a slippery rayon springtime print that molded her figure like water over boulders. Her nails were painted red, like poker chips. She seemed excited. "I hope you're hungry."

I nodded. I was famished.

I saw Kim look down at my hands, still filthy from my afternoon of larceny. "You didn't go to church," she said.

"Ricky and I got stoned. We also drank some ale and pawned some things."

The first step to repentance is confession.

"Well, get yourself cleaned up. I washed your white shirt and put it on your bed. Ricky pawned *whose* things?"

"Your twin's."

Kim buffed her nails on her sleeve and said, "I told her there was more to life than buying new appliances on time. I swear it's half the reason she got married: to double her credit limit. Oh, well. By the way, you had a phone call."

"Who?" Nobody knew where I was.

"He didn't give his name. All he said was, 'I'm a friend and I'll be back in touch.' "

Lucas—it had to be Lucas. I wondered how he'd tracked me down. Or maybe it was Conrad Burns, wondering what had happened to the pallet of fabric softener he'd fronted me a month ago. Whoever it was, it was best to ignore him. It was high time I moved on from that old crowd.

I crossed to the kitchen sink to wash my hands, and Kim said over my shoulder, "I'll give them my news when I'm ready, okay? Tonight, let's have a pleasant evening out. It's been a long time and I want to start slow."

"Whatever you think is best," I said, turning on the faucet. When the water was as hot as I could get it, I drenched my hands in liquid Ivory soap, enough to do a whole sinkful of dishes. I rubbed my hands together hard, rinsed off, then covered them in soap again. No use. My hands were dirty for good this time.

Mr. Lindgren ("Call me Chuck, it's faster") must have had firm, impressive muscles once, but what he had now was muscle-shaped fat stuffed inside a yellow polo shirt and a needlessly crushing handshake.

"Weaver, we're happy to have you," he said. "We're happy to have you both. Just thrilled."

We lowered ourselves into facing La-Z-Boys, a nervous mirror move. The other Lindgrens had disappeared, ex-

cusing themselves to get ready for dinner. Suddenly, it
was just us two.

"It's nice to be out of the city," I said. "It's so much
more relaxing here."

Chuck nodded as if he agreed, then said, "How come?
People always say such things, but I realize I have no idea
what they mean."

I didn't have an answer. I just sat there. Chuck was
using his open palms to smooth away the creases in his
violet dress slacks. The creases seemed to be hurting him,
as if they pointed in, not out; I sensed he was unaccus-
tomed to wearing ironed clothes. When the creases had
been sufficiently erased, he fiddled with his watch, a new-
looking chronograph model whose wealth of buttons and
small inner dials appeared to baffle him completely. Eventually, he roused himself and said, "According to my
daughter, you're a salesman."

"Yes. I mean, I used to be. At the moment, however,
I'm in between—"

"That's just fine," said Chuck. "There's nothing wrong,
in our age of many options, with trying lots of different
jobs. It's practically the norm, from what I hear."

Since Chuck seemed determined to think the best of
me, I decided to let him. Our chairs were deep and ex-
cessively padded, and I thought if we sat in them long
enough the tension between us would have to ease. I was
still waiting for that to happen when Chuck took a pack
of gum from his slacks, shuffled out two sticks, and passed
me one. We sat for a time in silence, chewing our Juicy
Fruit, floating out in space.

Chuck landed first. "She's a lovely girl, my daughter."

"Yes. She is."

He patted the side of his La-Z-Boy. "In case you didn't

know, there's a button down here if you want a massage."
He pressed his button and began to rumble, blurring ever
so slightly at the edges. I smiled, but declined to activate
my own chair.

Chuck leaned forward, frowning. He plucked out the
wad of gum from his mouth and set it on his knee, then
reconsidered and kept it in his hand. "I want to be clear
on something," he said, his voice picking up a tremor
from the chair. "My daughter's name is Agnes. In private,
you call her whatever you please—baby doll, little chip-
munk, whatever—but in front of my wife, it's Agnes.
Check?"

"Yes. Of course."

Chuck settled back in his chair and sighed, apparently
hugely relieved. "Sorry," he said, "but it's a husband's
duty. Consider all the arguments, all the competing points
of view, then side with your wife no matter what."

We shared an awkward, knowing laugh that concluded
when Chuck said, "Women. I tell you. Mothers, daugh-
ters, girlfriends, wives. You have to love them, don't you?
Ain't no choice."

I was desperate to change the subject. There was nothing I could contribute to this. I wondered if it would be
impolite to ask Chuck how much he'd won at Caesars
Palace.

Before I could open my mouth, he said, "We worried
about the poor girl, of course. She never wrote or telephoned. Couldn't be bothered, I guess. That's artists for
you. But now we see she's fine, and all's forgiven." He
smiled at me. "You two are friends."

I nodded.

Chuck said, "Good friends?"

I shrugged. He could think whatever he wanted to.

"Glad to hear it," he said. "Until you're a father your-self, you won't know how glad. I used to lay awake nights, afraid she'd taken up with some bohemian, some layabout finger-painter. It would have been a shame. That girl has the mark of a champion breeder, it's there in the shape of her chest, let's be honest. The thought of her suckling some scrawny hippie brood was more than I could take." He pinched at his slacks, as if to bring the crease back, then reached down and stilled the noisy La-Z-Boy. "What do you say we go eat now, really stuff our faces? Drink some wine."

"Fine with me." The image of Kim as a prize milk cow was something I couldn't get away from soon enough.

Once again, I mirrored Chuck as he stood up from his chair. He reached around to one of his back pockets and brought out a shocking, massive roll of bills. "It just doesn't figure," he said. "I work my whole life providing for others, and then when there's nobody left to provide for, I yank some silly handle and . . ." He looked at me, blank, as if I could explain this.

"I'm sure you deserve every penny," I said.

Chuck slipped the money back in his slacks and but-toned the pocket. He patted the bulge. "You're goddamn right I do."

We trooped down the path to Chuck and Dixie's car, falling into line according to our ages. As I passed the barn, it struck me that in the time I had been here, I hadn't heard a single cow noise or seen a single chore done. I mentioned this in a whisper to Ricky and asked if his folks were retired. "Don't have to retire," he said. "The farm's on set-aside. It's a government program that pays them good money to let the weeds take over."

Once we were all in the car—Chuck and Dixie up front, sitting with a space between them, and Ricky and Kim and I squeezed into the back—Chuck held a vote on which restaurant to go to. It had to be fancy, he said, and it had to serve seafood. Any suggestions? Ricky pushed hard for the Fargo Red Lobster, but Dixie said, "Forget it. That's a chain." Besides a chilly "Pleased to meet you," these were the first words I'd heard out of Dixie. I wondered if there was something wrong with her—uncomfortable shoes, perhaps, or a minor illness.

The restaurant we finally chose, a Fargo supper club, Trident's Grotto, was Dixie's idea, and it passed without debate. Her husband may have been steering the car, but she was driving it. That seemed fine with him.

The moon stayed put in the corner of the windshield as we rode along. The pot had worn off and left me tired and warm. Ricky fell asleep, his elbow jamming my kidney. Kim, on the other side of me, sat quiet and upright, her hands in her lap. Every few miles, Chuck would glance around the car as though to make sure we were all still inside it. A couple of times our eyes met in the rearview; Chuck smiled at me, I nodded back. After our chat in the living room, he seemed to regard me as a confidant, his backseat lieutenant. I felt flattered.

The waitress had started naming the specials when Chuck cut her off with a wave of his hand.

"One of each," he said. "Bring them all. Tonight the Lindgrens eat nothing but specials—as long as we men get plenty of shrimp!"

Dixie put down her menu and said, presumably to me, the stranger, "Chuck has this shrimp thing. He thinks they bring vigor."

"They're one big muscle," said Chuck, "they have to!"

Ricky said, "That's a fallacy," and slurped his whiskey sour. He didn't say *what* was a fallacy, but simply having used the word lent him an air of triumph. He set down his glass and said, "Agnes looks terrific. Don't you think so, Dixie? I do."

Dixie stirred her Mariner's Lament, an elaborate cocktail with three distinct levels: purple, blue, and green. "What matters is how the girl *feels*," she said. "I used to look terrific, too."

Chuck took a sudden interest in his chronograph, pushing all the buttons. Kim, who was drinking ice water— an encouraging touch of self-discipline, I thought— turned to her mother and said, "So why not *ask* me? Wouldn't that be simpler?"

"Ask you what, dear?"

"How I'm feeling."

Dixie said, frowning, "Because I'm waiting, Agnes. For you to ask me and your father how *we* feel."

The waitress came with the appetizer tray, and Chuck made a huge performance of passing it around. I suspected that Kim was crying as he spooned seafood salad onto her plate, but it was too dark to tell. Our table was way at the back of the grotto, next to a wall of rough, knobby plaster presumably meant to imitate a reef. A fishing net loaded with conch shells drooped to within a foot of our heads. The only light was a blue ship's lantern.

If only we'd gone to Red Lobster, I thought, where everyone could see each other's faces and Dixie would have to take responsibility for making her daughter cry.

By the time the waitress cleared the tray, though, I felt the gloom beginning to lift. Now that they had traded words, Kim and Dixie relaxed with each other. They talked about Las Vegas—the comedians Dixie had seen there, the magicians. Dixie lost her frown, describing them; the angle of her chin grew less severe. She had just launched into a full-blown description of Barry Manilow's concert act when a bottle of Chablis arrived and Chuck filled our glasses.

He proposed a toast: "To friends and family. The rich black topsoil of human happiness."

We all clinked goblets, except for Kim, who merely lifted her glass an inch or two off the table.

Chuck settled back in his chair and said, "Dixie, we're winners. And not just at slots. We're winners at life, which is far more important."

"I suppose that's true," she said, and burped. She fluttered her hand in front of her mouth, dispersing the vapors, then burped again. It made her human to me.

Chuck gave in to mellowness. "Kids, it's been a long, long haul, but your mother and I have cherished every moment. If we could, we'd do it all again."

I looked at Kim to see if she was listening. She was. This was an important speech for her.

"You bet," said Chuck. "We'd do it all again. And though I can see my wife over there about to say, 'Speak for yourself, you old fart, I want to go to Honolulu'—"

I glanced across at Dixie and saw that Chuck was right.

"—I know she agrees wholeheartedly," he said. "I know because . . . Ricky, that face you're making. Save it."

Ricky shrugged and poured himself more wine.

Dixie said, "Chuck, you're embarrassing our guest. Everyone understands your drunken sentiments."

Chuck looked at me. "I'm sorry, Weaver. Or are you just fine there?"

"I'm great, Chuck."

"Good," he said. "It's good you're great. I'm great, too. I'm perfect."

The seafood began to arrive, whole shoals full. The shrimp were the size of Chuck's thumbs, and there were dozens of them. A large fillet of sole afloat in a puddle of lemon butter was placed on a fold-out stand beside the table. There were scallops in red sauce, broiled lobster tails, platters of fried baby clams, and more Chablis. Chuck pulled a face after each new delivery, rolling back his eyes and saying, "Mercy," while Ricky gripped his knife and fork, waiting for the starting gun.

Kim picked up a spoon and struck her glass. "Before we start eating, I'd like you all to know—"

I froze.

It wasn't time yet.

This was wrong.

"—that my name is Kim, not Agnes. Beginning right now, when someone says Agnes, I will assume they're calling a dog. Is that understood, Mom?"

Dixie sipped her wine.

"Or should I just get up and leave?" Kim said. "Bev's wedding reception, part two."

Dixie put down her glass and said, "*Agnes* was a principle. A woman gives birth to a baby girl, launders her diapers, goes months without sleep, and for her trouble she gets to name the baby after her own beloved mother. But now I'm just too old for principles. I'd rather enjoy the rest of my life, *Kim*."

Dixie touched her salad fork and everyone dug in.

By the time we finished dinner, I had learned a lot about the Lindgrens. First, that they were selfish people and didn't like to share. Instead of passing the platters around and serving the person next to them, they would lunge forward and serve themselves first, hoarding their favorite dishes. Chuck took almost all the shrimp, Ricky got the lobster tails, and Dixie claimed most of the sole. I also learned that the Lindgrens were dishonest. Dixie, who seemed to be gulping her wine, told a story about Las Vegas and how she had lured a Japanese man away from the casino's hottest slot machine. She did this by dropping some money on the floor, and when the man bent down to pick it up, Dixie moved in and won six hundred dollars. Ricky, when he heard this, said, "Way to get those Japs, Dix," and Chuck sat back and beamed. There was more dishonesty when the waitress brought our bill, and Chuck said he wouldn't pay for the scallops because they tasted spoiled. The truth was we were just too full to eat them.

Like Ricky's "errands," the cheating didn't bother me. Instead, I felt privileged to be let in on it, as if it made me an honorary Lindgren. When the waitress crossed the scallops off our bill, Chuck gave the table a great big wink, and the only one who did not wink back was Kim, who gave her father a strict look. She turned a similar look on me—for letting Chuck off the hook, I assumed—but it was hardly necessary. I knew already that I was falling and Kim was rising, gaining strength.

Fortunately, she seemed to forgive me on the ride back home, letting her bare left knee brush my hand and leaving it pressed there over every bump. Dixie and Ricky yawned and dozed while Chuck hummed along with a country station. Because Midwesterners can't digest seafood, there was a lot of polite, suppressed belching. I even heard Kim belch once or twice. And that's when I knew

I wanted to stay here and not go back to St. Paul for a while. Because when Kim belched, then excused herself, and I belched back and Chuck did, too, the circle felt complete and good to be in. I thought I had found my own people. At last.

Fifteen

I slept in the guest room that night and the next. Kim
crept in at dawn both mornings and sat on the edge of
my bed, looking pale and tired and sick, until she felt
able to vomit. She would return from the bathroom saying
she was much, much better but looking only a little better,
and for the next hour or so, while the others in the house
remained asleep, we would sit and hold hands and whisper in the dark. I knew that something was happening to
me, happening to both of us, but I did not know what to
do about it. My Bible was there beside us, on the bedstand,
and once or twice I opened it at random and read a few
verses aloud and prayed for guidance. Kim listened to my
prayers but didn't join them. I didn't ask her to.

I had given up trying to convert her.

I had my own flawed soul to consider.

The second morning we talked about Kim's pregnancy, but only in code, as "the situation," and not for long, because she got so frustrated. She said she had tried to break the news to Dixie, but couldn't get the words out. I asked her what she was afraid of.

"I don't know. Putting a crimp in her golden years."

"Isn't she curious why you came home?"

Kim said, "No. She thinks she knows: because I couldn't make it in St. Paul. Because I'm a helpless, pathetic air-head who—"

I squeezed her hand and said, "Stop that talk. Why don't you go to your father?"

"Chuck's in another world. All he does is play with that dumb watch and think how he's going to spend his big winnings."

We walked on the farm later that morning while Chuck and Dixie went shopping in Fargo. They were being cagey about how much money they'd won, but Ricky claimed to have seen a cashier's check for $62,000. The sum seemed fantastically high to me, but then I knew nothing about Las Vegas and what sort of things were possible there. I remembered my mother telling me once that she and my father used to go there before I was born, when they were young and wild. Perhaps because I couldn't envision her ever being young and wild, Las Vegas had never seemed real to me, either. I pictured it as a kind of Hell-town, permanently bathed in flames, where anxious souls who lacked the patience to wait for Judgment Day went to preview their ultimate luck.

Kim and I followed a cow path down through the thistle-choked pasture into a shady hollow of woods where the ground was bare and flat and sandy. Kim said that when she was small, she liked to camp out overnight in the spot and imagine herself as a Cheyenne brave tracking Custer's army. I asked her if she and Bev had ever played Cheyenne braves together. Kim laughed and said, "Bev liked indoor games. Teddy-bear tea parties, Ken and Barbie's wedding. *Girl* shit."

As we were talking, Ricky showed up. He sat on a log drinking an ale and raving about the recession, portraying it as a Wall Street plot to bankrupt small businesses, then buy them out. He worked himself into such a foul mood that Kim had to tell him to leave. An hour later, we spotted him in the pasture, pacing the fence line and moving his lips, apparently holding a fierce one-man debate. Kim said he had always been this way: serious, dissatisfied, accusatory. She said that when he was a teenager, he used to spit at the television set whenever it broadcast footage of the president. If Hinckley had not been charged with shooting Reagan, she would have suspected her brother, she said.

Kim talked about her parents, too. When she left home four years ago, she said, Chuck and Dixie were always fighting—fighting over money, over chores, over where to travel on vacations that, when it was time to go, they always found some excuse to back out of. But now, she said, they seemed happier together—duller, fatter, lazier, but happier. They didn't wake up as early as they used to or turn out the lights when they left a room. And Kim had a feeling, she said, that her parents planned to move away soon, perhaps to the Gulf Coast of Florida, where so many of their friends had ended up. She said that when she'd passed their room last night, she had heard Dixie urging Chuck to spend a chunk of their gambling winnings on a new RV.

"You have to tell them soon," I said.

Kim said, "Maybe I can't. Maybe you should," and looked at me with forlorn, hopeful eyes.

"It's not my place," I said.

"It's not? Then what are you doing here, Weaver? This whole pointless visit was your idea, not mine. Remember: *The happy farmers reunite*."

That hurt, and Kim knew it.

She apologized.

On our walk around the farm, I learned that avoiding a big thing helps you to focus on very small things. The big thing was Kim's condition; the small things were deer tracks behind the house, the drone of far-off farm machinery, the red-tailed hawks that circled high above us. The animal life and the wide blue sky put me in a mood to talk about myself. I told Kim about my mother the businesswoman, and how, on my sixteenth birthday, she gave me a thousand-dollar bank account and a pamphlet explaining how compound interest worked. I told Kim I'd spent the money on drugs and record albums, and that, when my mother found out what I'd done, she sent me to a psychiatrist friend who tested my personality. The psychiatrist said I had inner hostility, narcissism, and other problems, and that I needed therapy. My mother decided he charged too much, though, and enrolled me in judo lessons instead.

I demonstrated a couple of kicks, the only judo moves I could remember. Kim seemed impressed. She said I had good reflexes.

I kissed her.

That was as far as it went, though: one kiss. Kim would have let me go further, I knew, but suddenly I felt dizzy again, as if I were going to be sick myself, and I broke the hug. I wondered if I had made a mistake by not going back to St. Paul. The problem was there was nothing there I missed, and no one whom I could imagine missing me. I *wanted* to miss things—my church friends, my apartment—but when I tried to see them in my mind and work up some feeling about them, nothing happened, which made me sad. It made me sad that in all my time down there, from working at Hidden Planet to riding around in the Conscience Squad school bus to selling Sanipure, I had never established a life for myself.

After our kiss and the interrupted hug we sat in the grass and had another talk.

Kim said, "I have to know something, Weaver. What are you going to do once I tell them?"

"That depends," I said, "on what they say."

"Why does it depend?"

"What if they want you to stay?"

Kim said, "Believe me, they won't. They're booked on too many Caribbean cruises."

I feared she was right and couldn't speak. I remembered her dream of the disappearing ocean liner.

Kim said, "Say they throw me out. What then? What's your contingency plan for that one?"

I plucked some grass and tore it into pieces.

"Listen, it's simple," she said. "Are you my boyfriend now, or not? I don't need a moral guardian, Weaver. I can watch Pat Robertson for that."

Our conversation went on like this—breaking off in ultimatums, resuming with leading questions, pausing for hugs, dissolving into tears. We were talking in circles and walking in them, too. The only clear thing that came out of it all was that Kim was going crazy, and I was at fault. I might have to leave soon, she said, or she might have to. Maybe she didn't want this baby after all, or maybe she would give birth to it alone, anonymously, in another city.

Everything was a mess.

Then Kim fell down.

We were crossing a barbed-wire fence when it happened. Kim said the fall was my fault, but I thought it was hers. I was lifting the top strand of wire to keep it from snagging her shirt as she climbed through. I looked away for a moment to watch what I thought was a big buck deer grazing in the distance. The next thing I knew Kim was flat on the ground. I reached out my hand to help her up, but she refused to take it. There was dirt all over the front of her shirt and a small jagged scratch on her chin. She stood and touched her chin and looked at the blood, then looked at me. Her eyes were ugly, fierce.

"That was on purpose," she said.

I stood there.

"Why did you trip me?" she said. "You tripped me!"

"You tripped yourself."

Kim threw up her hands and turned and walked off. She stopped a few yards away and stood there, frozen. I did not move, either, and it hit me that we could stay this way for hours or days or weeks, and that maybe this was the best situation a man and a woman could hope for: to stand a short distance off from each other, never budging, almost touching, not quite separate and not quite together.

Kim broke the silence. "I want to see a doctor. I have to know what's going on with me. Maybe it's hormonal change."

"Fine," I said. "Of course. Which doctor?"

"My fucking *family* doctor."

"Please don't curse."

"And you're coming with me," she said. "You're going to talk to him, too."

"When?"

"Now. This minute. I'm exploding."

We headed for my car.

At the clinic's front desk an elderly nurse gave Kim a clipboard with forms to fill out. Kim said she didn't need the forms—that Dr. Muntz was a family friend and already knew her medical history. The nurse said, "These are insurance forms, dear," and Kim said, "I don't *have* insurance. Just go back and tell the doctor Agnes Lindgren's here. The pinky girl."

The nurse disappeared down a hallway. Kim and I sat on the waiting-room sofa next to a man with tubes in his nose that ran to a portable oxygen tank. I asked Kim what "pinky girl" meant. She held her left hand up and said, "A sickle got it." She showed me a faint red scar just above the second joint. "We put it on ice and drove it to the hospital and Dr. Muntz reattached it. That's his specialty: farm-related injuries."

I thought: *For once, a surgeon who replaces things instead of removing them.*

When Dr. Muntz appeared in the waiting room, Kim went straight to him, into his arms. Right there, I liked the man. He was sixty years old, perhaps, and very tall, with white buzz-cut hair, big red Dumbo ears, and deep sun-cracked lines in his forehead. He struck me as the sort of rugged, kind physician whose lab-coat pockets are always stuffed with sweets—who spends his vacations in places like El Salvador inoculating refugee camps. While he and Kim stood there catching up, I leafed through a copy of *Highlights for Children*, absently working the puzzles, finding the hidden words. The phrase in my head was: *Good hands. She's in good hands.*

I turned a page of the magazine and suddenly I felt useless, obsolete. My mission finished.

Then I heard Kim say, "Weaver, will you wait?"

I lifted my head and said, "Yes. Of course."

The doctor smiled at me. "If you'd like some coffee or tea, young man, my nurse should be back in a moment."

Kim said, "I'm sorry, I should have introduced you. Dr. Muntz, this is my boyfriend, Weaver Walquist."

I stood to shake the doctor's hand. My body felt strangely light. Not just unheavy, but light, as in energy. It was Kim's introduction that had done it.

Her calling me her boyfriend made it true.

"You two take your time," I said. "I'll be fine out here."

I had exhausted three issues of *Highlights*, a government pamphlet on diabetes (our leading preventable cause of blindness), and a six-month-old copy of *Newsweek* when the doctor returned to the waiting room, said to the nose-tube man, "Hang in there, Elmer," and asked me to come down the hall to his office. As we passed a series of ancient public-service posters on the dangers of "uppers," "downers," and "smack," the doctor informed me that Kim had been examined by the clinic's gynecologist and now was being X-rayed in case she had injured herself in her fall. He pointed me to the stool by his desk and leaned against the examination table.

He crossed his arms. "Your girlfriend and I had a good long talk. She's ten weeks pregnant, thereabouts. The biological father, I'm told, is not in the picture. Good riddance, it seems. She suffers acutely from morning sickness, but otherwise she's in perfect health."

"That's good news," I said.

The doctor frowned. "I may as well be honest, Mr. Walquist. I distrust your type. Not you—your type."

I asked him which type that was, expecting one of the usual answers: bigots, kooks, gestapos.

"Young American males," the doctor said. "The most dangerous age, the most dangerous sex, living in the most dangerous country. Demographically speaking, you're trouble. The army, the jails, the psych wards—those are your natural homes."

I was stunned. I watched the doctor reach into his lab coat and bring out a pack of Camels and a lighter.

"I hope it doesn't shock you that I smoke. We doctors don't always take our own advice. I believe there's a Bible verse to that effect."

I held two fingers against my lips to signal I wanted a cigarette myself. I don't know why I did it. Perhaps I just wanted to throw the doctor off and complicate his picture of me. Kim must have told him I was born-again, and people have fixed ideas about us that it is sometimes helpful to refute. Or maybe I was just nervous. In any case, I took a cigarette and the doctor lit it for me, flicking his Zippo like an old-time barkeep.

The doctor said, "Agnes—Kimberly—asked me to have a few words with you about your intentions toward her. Actually, it was quite a scene in here. You should be very proud of yourself. You've done quite a job on her head."

"That's not fair," I said. "All I did was point out certain—"

"Be honest. It was a scare campaign."

"A truth campaign."

"You know, it's always puzzled me," he said, "why you people set out to rescue beings who are basically invisible to you. A craving for nobility? For chivalric purpose?"

"To me, they're not invisible. I see them. I actually see them. In color."

"Mania is a treatable condition."

"They used to call it 'having a conscience.'"

The doctor spoke right over me. "Do you feel romantic affection for her, Weaver, or is she just a moral homework project? A focus for your odd delusions? The girl's my patient, I have a right to know."

I looked at the stethoscope around his neck and thought of the curled-up snake on the pole that symbolizes medicine. I had always suspected that snake of being poisonous. "Yes," I said, "I feel affection for her. What I don't feel any affection for is murdering innocent babies."

"Why's that?"

His casualness startled me. "Because," I said, "it's a sin. It's murder. It's ruining lives and poisoning our nation. If people could only see the fetus—"

"I have," the doctor said. "I've seen."

"I'm sorry. I meant if the public could." I felt my earlobes burning.

"Let's forget the public for a moment and concentrate on you," the doctor said. "Kim says you're uncomfortable with her. She feels you're rejecting her physically. Why?"

I described for him some of my Christian beliefs, but not, I feared, with much force or passion. He listened to me, as nonbelievers do, with an expression of mixed respect and puzzlement. When I finished my speech, he dragged on his Camel and let the smoke leak out his nose and roll down the front of his lab coat. "That is all quite admirable," he said, "but it's nothing to found an adult romance on. Kimberly wants an adult romance."

"Adult romance," I said. "I can't say I know what that is, exactly. You mean like on the soap operas?"

The doctor's voice was flat. "I'm not surprised you don't know what romance is. From what Kim has told me, it's clear you've never had one."

If the doctor had not sewn Kim's fingertip back on, I might have snapped back at him then or left his office. Instead, I sat there and waited to hear more. He had performed one impossible feat; perhaps he could perform another.

"Let's get our terms straight," the doctor said. "First: Are you a virgin?"

"No, I'm not."

"Is it intercourse you object to or sexual activity in general? Penetration or all stimulation?"

I coughed on smoke. "Could you slow down, please?"

The doctor said, "Don't brood, just answer. Self-consciousness isn't the point here. Knowledge is."

"It's more like penetration," I said.

"The thought of it, or the sensation?"

"Both. The thought *of* the sensation."

"What else?"

"Erections," I said.

"What about them?"

It was rapid-fire now.

"They hurt."

"Physically?"

"Spiritually."

That stopped him.

He stubbed out his cigarette, lit another. Waited.

"I trained myself not to have them," I said. I checked the doctor's face for a reaction.

He didn't even blink, he just said, "How? Some crude aversion therapy?"

A novocaine numbness filled my jaw. The method I had been taught at church along with so many other single men was by no means a secret, and yet it felt sacrilegious to reveal it. Or perhaps the method itself was sacrilegious. To know, I would have to speak up and let it out.

"I learned it from a book," I said. "A book my pastor recommended. I think it was called *Achieving Purity*."

The doctor blew smoke out one side of his mouth.

"When you get an erection . . . ," I said.

"Go on, son."

"You imagine Our Lord on the cross. His wounds."

"That's monstrous."

I looked at the floor and felt the tears well. "And then your erection . . . subsides."

"Yes," the doctor said. "I'm sure it would."

I sat there feeling smaller and weaker than I had ever felt as the doctor came over and held my shoulder and thanked me for my candor. The laying-on of hands was common at the Bryce Street Church of God, but this was the first time I ever felt it working. Pastor Spannring's touch was nowhere near as calming as the doctor's, perhaps because the pastor's touch came with strings attached. Even if you did not feel healed by him, you were obliged to say you did, often before a crowd.

Here, all I had to do was sit and breathe.

All I had to do was feel the hand.

Some time passed and I looked back up. Kim stood in the doorway to the office, clutching her X-ray film to her chest the way young girls hold schoolbooks. The doctor clipped the X-rays to a light-board, then turned off the fluorescent ceiling lamp. We stood together in the darkened office, gazing at Kim's insides. We could see the ribs, the heart, the outlines of the lungs. I dried my eyes with a tissue from the desk to get a clearer view, then heard the doctor say from the shadows, "I'd like to see the two of you next week, but for now just try to be good to each other. The pictures are normal."

I looked at Kim, who said, "Good," looking at me. The light from the X-ray board was cool and diffuse, like moonlight, and covered half her face, leaving the other half in darkness. She whispered, "Thank you, Weaver. You were right. I can see it, too, now."

I fell in love with her then.

Sixteen

WE DID NOT RETURN TO THE FARM THAT DAY, OR FOR THAT matter, ever again. Kim let me know as we drove away from the clinic that she was no longer welcome there. She said she had telephoned Chuck and Dixie from Dr. Muntz's office, informed them of her pregnancy, and been told in no uncertain terms that she was on her own.

"They didn't sound angry, just firm," she said. "They said we can stay at my sister's house—apparently, Chuck holds the mortgage on the place. We have to pay utilities and upkeep. Bev's not coming back."

"Why not?"

"Typical white-trash melodrama. Not worth getting into."

"Did your parents say anything else?"

"That's it," said Kim. "No more Agnes. Free at last. I have to admit, though, my dad *was* kind of sweet."

"Sweet in what way?"

"About the baby. He said we'd have a big one. Heavy birthweight. You know, farmer talk."

I stared out the windshield. "He thinks it's mine."

"Well, isn't it?"

Ricky was on the front porch when we pulled into Bev's driveway. He lay stretched out on a beat-up lawn chair, its nylon webbing frayed and flyaway, reading a book called *Beat the Elite—Resisting the Trilateralist Conspiracy*. When Kim approached the porch steps, he hustled up out of the chair and took her by the elbow, treating her like an invalid—as if she were eight months pregnant instead of just two and a half. He said he had been in the room when she'd called home and had heard the whole thing.

"I've had it with those two—I'm out of there. I'll pick up our stuff tomorrow. The *bastards*."

Kim lifted Ricky's hand off her arm and asked him where he planned to stay.

"I'll sleep in the van," he said. "I'll park it out back, so it won't be a nuisance. Give you two your privacy."

Ricky went on to offer Kim more sympathy and rant about Chuck and Dixie's cruelty, but she refused to be drawn in. Instead, she went straight to work rearranging Bev's house to her liking. I shadowed her with the dustpan and the Windex bottle as she fussed and cleaned, but I was too numb to be of much help. Her parents, I felt, had acted shamefully, and I was embarrassed at how I'd misjudged them. I knew from their table manners they were selfish, but I had not expected such disloyalty.

Kim, however, seemed exhilarated to have a place of

her own again. Considering what had happened to her last place, I could understand. She scoured the sinks and the bathtub with Ajax, pushed a dust mop along the baseboards, then started in on the children's bedroom. She moved in a card table and a desk lamp and set out pencils and paper. "I have to get back to my cards," she said. "First thing tomorrow, no excuses." When she finished in the kids' room, she made a last pass through the rest of the house, changing bedclothes, straightening rugs, taking down pictures she said were vulgar, and generally putting her mark on all she touched. When she reached the living room, I realized I had better pitch in soon or risk becoming dead weight in her eyes. I moved the sofa and rocker-recliner, positioned to face the pawned TV set, into a conversational circle.

For dinner, I threw together a casserole from some of the canned goods Bev had left in the kitchen cupboard. I served the meal on the porch. Perhaps to reward herself for her hard work, Kim took the lawn chair; Ricky and I sat cross-legged on the floor. Outlined against the orange sunset, Kim looked to me like a queen up there, an empress. She had a new air of entitlement, nobility, as if she were already set to claim the privileges traditionally accorded motherhood. I couldn't take my eyes off her. She praised my casserole, Ricky echoed her, and except for the noisy muffler of a car that passed by slowly on the county road, then turned and drove back the way it came, there was no other sound for the rest of the meal.

Kim and I shared a bed that night, but all we did was lie there. She seemed to fall asleep instantly—I may not have slept at all. My dream, if it really was a dream and not just a case of losing track of time, was of lying on a mattress with a woman under a mothball-smelling sheet and trying to keep from falling out of bed. The only dream-like thing about it was that the floor was a lake or an ocean—some kind of body of water, with waves. To avoid falling in, I nudged the woman, pushed against her hip with my hip. The woman didn't budge. Indeed, the more I pushed, the closer I seemed to come to the edge and the louder the sound of the waves grew.

The struggle seemed to go on for hours, although it was only a struggle on my side, since all the woman did was lie there and expand. The effort made me thirsty, desperate for a drink. I saw a glass of water on the bedside table, but when I tried to reach for it, I found that I couldn't lift my left arm, which was hanging out over the edge of the mattress.

I heard myself say, "You're asleep. You're not awake yet," and then I really did wake up, I thought. Only this time my arm had been amputated; my shoulder was a bloody stump. I shut my eyes and opened them again, and suddenly there was sunlight everywhere and I was down at the foot of the bed, snarled in the sheets and drenched in sweat.

I heard Kim saying: "Come here. It's just a dream. Everything's all right."

I glanced at the floor and saw carpet, not ocean. I crawled up next to Kim, still testing my awakeness. She cuddled me for a while and soon I was cuddling her back. She pulled her T-shirt off over her head and twisted around at the waist, presenting her bra strap to me.

It took me a moment to know what Kim was asking. She said, "Go ahead. Don't think, just do." I undid the hooks with my missing hand, the one that had miraculously grown back. Kim held her arms up. I slid the bra off.

The rest of it was just following instructions.

Later that morning, Kim and I had sex again.

We had to.

Otherwise, I might never have stopped crying.

The tears started falling just after the first time, when Kim snatched a Kleenex tissue from the nightstand and wiped it around the place on her stomach where I had had my orgasm. Once she had dried herself off, she got out of bed without looking at me and went into the bathroom and shut the door. I heard the shower turn on. I touched the swollen red end of my penis; it seemed to have grown since I had last used it. That was the thought that made me start crying: "Where have you been for all this time?"

Dressing helped me pull myself together. Zipping my fly was a great relief. I waited for Kim to come out of the bathroom, planning to hold her and say soft things and do what a man should do after sex according to the books and magazines. That was the world I felt I had come back to: *How to Please Her. The Playboy Advisor. Your Romantic Horoscope.* When I heard the shower stop, I said, "How long are you going to be in there?"

"A while."

"I love you," I said in my new magazine voice.

"You're sweet," said Kim. "Have Ricky make some coffee."

I broke down again after breakfast. Kim had gone into her studio to work, and Ricky was at the sink doing dishes. Actually, there were no dishes, just some plastic-coated paper plates that the package claimed were washable.

Ricky took the label at its word, but the plates turned soggy and fell apart when he passed them under the faucet. I remembered a high-school social-studies teacher who had lectured my class one day concerning "our disposable society." I was not sure at the time what he meant: that society was disposable, or that it was full of disposable things? I decided, watching Ricky toss the plates out and thinking of Kim's Kleenex, that there was no real difference.

Because I did not have a life anymore, meaning a job or a church, I could have done practically anything that day: planted a garden, contemplated cloud forms, circulated Dakota First petitions. All of a sudden, my options seemed unlimited, and I was terrified. I finished my fourth or fifth cup of instant coffee and wandered into Kim's studio to see if she needed help with anything.

She had her back to me, writing. The wicker wastebasket next to her chair overflowed with crumpled sheets of yellow legal paper. At her elbow I saw a paperback thesaurus. I made a small noise to announce my presence. Kim turned around with a startled expression.

"More coffee?" I said.

"I'm fine," Kim said. "It's kind of hard getting started, but I'm fine."

"If there's something you'd like me to read . . . If you need feedback . . ." Another magazine word.

Kim said no.

Turning to leave the room, I said, "I'm sorry. I didn't mean to intrude on your work."

Kim got the message and came to me, putting her arms around my neck and gazing up from the two-inch disadvantage that, by some odd coincidence, all my past girlfriends had shared. "I'm happy," she said. "It was nice this morning. Warm. I think we're good together."

The editors of *Playboy* would have known how to respond, but I did not. I gathered I had done well, but merely doing well was not a breakthrough. I had always done well with women, especially the first or second time. No, what I wanted to feel with Kim and wanted her to feel with me was something more than "nice" and "warm." I wanted to leap from one shore, faith, where it was dry and solid and safe, onto the other shore, ultimate sin, where we would sink down together into Hell and be fallen angels together, with horns. A slim ray of light would have to shine down then, God's promise to all sinners, and together we could repent and be one. Or never repent, and be one in another way.

Backsliding, unlike "adult romance" and the healthful "safe sex" of the magazines, was something I understood.

To do it right, you had to sin, not stumble.

It called for penetration, which Kim and I had avoided that morning.

A few minutes later we were back in bed, sitting against the chrome-and-glass headboard of Bev's ridiculous matching bedroom set. Kim worked her jeans off but kept her T-shirt on. Myself, I stripped naked immediately. Kim said, "You're cute. It's like you're going swimming," and reached across the bed and tickled my hand. I pulled away, uncomfortable with cuteness. I wanted to come at her from a distance and make her face up to all the stages—invasion, contact, capture—not like this morning's cuddly tumble.

What followed was a kind of fight. Whenever I moved in and gained some leverage, Kim would tickle me, poke at my soft spots, and force me to let go of her. I assumed that she wanted to lose the fight, although her sheer persistence made me wonder. At one point, I got the upper hand (we were on our sides, and face to face) by using a tricky schoolyard wrestling hold. That seemed to be just what she wanted—a slapstick tussle, mere fun—so I released her. When she started back in with the tickling, I let my whole body go slack and did not react.

Kim gave up and took her hands off me. "You're a lot of fun today."

For a moment, we didn't move, just faced each other. Then Kim said, "Whatever. Have it your way," and rolled on her back as if she'd lost interest. I rolled over, too.

There had to be dozens of ways to end the standoff, but one person always has to go first, and neither of us seemed willing to do that. I lay there with my eyes shut, seeing the changing shapes of every color that may be what you are really praying to when you think you are praying to God. Anger was rising up in me, real anger. Kim had set a trap for me, a snare, and I had walked right into it. Lying there with her arms crossed on her chest, she felt the same way about me, I suspected.

And then something happened. A kind of revelation. Proof that love does not require a winner—that there can be tie games, too.

Kim turned to me and I turned to her and our anger was equal. Our souls matched. I suppose they had matched all along without our knowing it, but now we could see that they did. Kim said, "Leave me alone, you jerk," and I said, "You leave me alone, you bitch," and then, together, one voice: "Come here."

Suddenly it felt to me as if we were free to do anything.

Be ourselves and also be each other's.

Perhaps even raise a child together.

We lay on our sides and faced each other and put our hands wherever it felt good, on ourselves and on the other person, and although there was no penetration because we agreed the time was not yet right, we were happy together, Kim and I, and satisfied afterward. Dr. Muntz would have been proud of us, I felt, and proud of me in particular. I was learning to be with another person, and not just another person, a woman. And not just any woman: Kim.

Then Lucas Boone showed up.

Seventeen

I WAS DOWN AT THE END OF THE DRIVEWAY, PUTTING A NOTE to my mother in the mailbox after a morning spent praying on the porch. According to Reverend Dale of "Positions," the purpose of prayer was not so much to gain your heart's desire as to find out what your heart's desire was. He said you should be specific in your prayers and not be concerned if they sounded petty. If what you truly wanted was a wide-screen Sony Trinitron TV—if you sincerely believed that such an item would make your life complete—then you should ask for exactly that, by brand name. Being vague and modest in your prayers either showed a lack of faith ("As if the Almighty shops on a budget!") or confusion about your true desires.

I had a good idea what I should pray for. Number one:

money. Enough to restock the kitchen cupboards, keep my gas tank full, and pay at least a token sum for Dr. Muntz's services. Number two: the inner strength to keep making love to Kim and not go haywire. Number three: acceptance for Kim's work. I couldn't say I understood her greeting cards, but I knew how important they were to her, and love, as I had begun to understand it, meant wanting for the other person what she wanted for herself. Also, I needed a job, but since I had no idea what sort of opportunities existed here in North Dakota, I prayed for general wisdom instead.

I raised the tin flag on the mailbox. The note to my mother was brief: "Send a thousand dollars. It's important. You have to trust me. Weaver." I could have explained my need for the money, but that would have taken pages and pages, and it was crucial the note go out immediately. We were down to bulk oatmeal and canned spaghetti and a box of Minute Rice. There was an overdue power bill. What's more, Kim had broken a window this morning while trying to get some fresh air in her studio. I'd tacked a sheet of plastic to the frame, but Kim deserved glass. She deserved a clear view. Also, I needed a set of plumbing tools to fix a drip in the master bathroom.

I started back toward the house, my head full of projects. I felt tired but hopeful. I liked it that the land up here was flat and I could see for miles in all directions. It matched my idea of my life now. Over the roof of the house, I saw a thin white contrail breaking up into puffs. I decided to spend the afternoon weeding the flowerbeds next to the garage. And then, behind me, I heard a car, and before I even turned around to look, I knew I had gotten ahead of myself.

* * *

Only someone who had known him well would have recognized Lucas Boone. He pulled alongside me in his filthy station wagon (someone had traced the words *Wash me* on the hood) and stopped and killed the engine. He looked terrible. His dandruffy dark eyebrows had wild swirls and peaks. The part in his hair, which once ran razor straight, wandered across his badly sunburned scalp like an undressed wound. The hand draped over the top of the steering wheel appeared to have been plunged in acid: flaking red skin, corroded nails. Worse, his entire shape had changed. His face and neck seemed drained of flesh, and their loss was his belly's gain. All that remained of his old Navy self was a gray short-sleeved shirt with epaulets. Its color matched the color of his cheeks.

"Been doing a lot of driving," he said. He jerked his thumb at the folded-down backseat and his rolled-out sleeping bag. "And camping."

"Oh," I said. "Hello." I couldn't think.

Lucas nodded and licked his windburned lips. For once, it seemed that he could not think either.

"My old friend Weaver," he said. "How are you?"

"Fine," I said. "Just fine. How did you find me here, Lucas?"

"I made some calls. Some inquiries. Your friends are very concerned about your whereabouts. Conrad Burns—"

"Can go jump in a lake."

Lucas said, "Clean break. I understand."

Next to him, on the seat, I saw a Holy Bible, open to one of the red-letter sections, possibly the Sermon on the Mount. "By the way, I paid your rent," he said. "I went to your apartment and caught your landlord hauling out your stuff. Don't worry, though, I covered it."

I checked my mental calendar and realized my rent was indeed overdue.

"I'll pay you back," I said. Then, to be polite: "And how are you?"

Lucas's nodding had turned into rocking. "Driving, camping, you know . . ." He gazed out his windshield, through the nicks and cracks.

I stood there, breathing.

"Trouble," he said softly. "So much trouble."

I took a judgmental pause and said, "I heard."

He stopped rocking and looked at me. He hadn't actually looked at me yet. This was the test, this moment. He had to confess or explain. I assumed he had enough respect for me to know I deserved nothing less. I also hoped he understood that if he chose to offer explanations, I was by no means obliged to accept them.

"I'm sorry," he said, and he faced me full-on. "This has been bad. Abominable. And no excuses. None. I put the girl in a terrible position. Put us all in one. And you, sir, you are entitled, *fully*, to hear the whole—"

My eyes took in the contents of the car: muddy backpack, snack-food wrappers, scattered dimes and pennies, a roll of toilet paper. Seeing them brought to mind the word *forsaken*. Justly forsaken, perhaps, but still forsaken. Adam banished, Cain cast out.

"Maybe later," I said. "Some other time."

I pitied the man.

I couldn't help it.

Lucas said, "I understand. I do."

"I'm busy. I'm sorry. We just moved in here."

"Ten minutes," Lucas said. "That's all."

I looked at the fields. I inhaled. Deep, deep breath.

"Ten or fifteen minutes."

Then I exhaled.

"Bless you, Weaver. Bless you."

Lucas sat at the kitchen table. I poured him a glass of tap water. I felt it was the least I could offer before I asked him to leave.

He downed the glass in one long gulp. He wiped his mouth with his hand and said, "You'd never know by this gut of mine, but I've been fasting. It's murder in this heat. The moisture flies right out of you."

I took his glass to the sink and refilled it. I opened the freezer compartment of the fridge. Only two cubes remained in the tray.

"Sorry, out of ice," I said.

Giving Lucas the last two of anything seemed to me unwarranted.

I turned and saw him nod at the refrigerator.

"Excuse me," he said, "but you need food. Cupboard's pretty bare there, Weaver. I hope you've been eating better than I have."

I said, "There are three of us." I don't why I said it; it didn't really answer his remark. Perhaps I just wanted Lucas to know that I had superior numbers on my side.

I watched him reach around to his back pocket and bring out four crisp twenty-dollar bills. He fanned them out on the table like playing cards. "A small contribution. For sundries," he said. "Believe me, I know how depressing empty shelves are. The day my wife left, she cleaned out the kitchen. Left me a cold cup of tea and a note."

I looked at the eighty dollars, remembering my morning

168

prayer for money. I had not expected an answer so soon. Or from such a dubious source.

"Pay me back whenever," Lucas said. "That's my new byword: whenever. Whatever. I think I'm becoming a fatalist, a Buddhist."

"A Buddhist," I said.

"In my situation a little Buddhism helps. Not literally, of course—I'm still a Christian—but as a coping aid. A calming agent. You know I was addicted to those things. Hopelessly addicted."

"What things?"

"Those damnable Prozacs. Those pills." He reached in his shirt pocket, looking for something, but couldn't seem to find it. "I have an article somewhere. A reprint from *Newsweek*. My lawyer gave it to me."

"Lucas, you need to talk quietly. My housemates . . ."

He whispered: "It's full of horror stories. Arsons, killings, suicides—all of them Prozac-related. Prozac-caused. This is it, I think . . ." From the credit-card compartment of his wallet, he drew out a tightly folded piece of paper. He unfolded it and passed it to me, nodding at the headline: "Psychosis in a Capsule?"

"Not that I blame the pills alone," he said. "Chemicals are chemicals, and human weakness is human weakness. Blaming what I did solely on some drug, that's like blaming . . . Oh, I don't know . . ."

I scanned the article's first few paragraphs. Lucas was being truthful: Prozac had a history. The word *paranoia*, underlined in pencil, recurred throughout the text. Also the phrase *aggressive episodes*. The photo in the middle of the page showed a certain "Janet Cox," described as "a depressed Ohio housewife," being handcuffed by police. Apparently, she had attacked her infant son while under

Prozac's influence. A jury had found her not guilty. I read further. There were other cases. Dozens of them.

Lucas said, "I repeat: No excuses. My only point is, drugs can warp your mind. Of course, you already know that. You've been there."

I heard a sound from off in the house: Kim standing up from her desk chair or Ricky coming in the back way. People were going to meet.

"Haven't you?" said Lucas.

"What?"

"Been there," he said. "With drugs. With pills . . . What's wrong?"

I was staring at Janet Cox, obviously a woman in pain. She resembled an older version of Kim. Similar figure. Same mouth.

"This article," I said. "It's sad."

Lucas said, "Something else you should know: Prozac was not going to be my defense. My lawyer pushed for it, I refused. Just ask him. If the girl hadn't dropped the charges to shield the church's name, I would have pled guilty. I'd be in prison now." He cast down his eyes at the floor and clasped his hands, so tightly I saw his knuckles whiten. "Jesus, Lord, who sees all, knows all, forgive me, that others may also forgive me, and I may forgive myself."

He lifted his face—the tears I saw seemed real.

They shocked me.

I heard another sound and said, "Pull yourself together. Someone's coming."

A moment later, Kim walked in. She nodded at us and went straight to the sink, apparently lost in thought. She set the pot on the stove and lit the gas.

I shoved the *Newsweek* article deep into my pants

pocket. My hand emerged shaking. "Kim, this is Lucas."

Lucas said, "It's nice to meet you, Kim."

Kim said, "Likewise. Hi. Weaver, where's the instant coffee? Ricky didn't drink it all, I hope."

Coffee, when Kim was at work, was not a luxury.

"I'm sorry," I said. "I did."

"*All* of it?"

"I'll buy some tomorrow."

"When tomorrow?"

"Early."

Lucas said, "That does it," and pushed back his chair and stood up. "As I was just telling Weaver, Kim, I need a few groceries myself. What can I get you? Coffee and what else?"

Kim said, "You're going out anyway?"

Lucas smiled. "I am."

"In that case—"

"Let's do this," said Lucas. "I'll use the bathroom while you make your list. And please don't skimp. It's a gift. I owe this kid."

Kim gave Lucas directions to the bathroom. When he was gone, she said, "He's nice. Who is he?" I saw her eye the twenties on the table.

"A guy," I said. "A church acquaintance."

"Is he staying? Looks exhausted."

"He's camping in the area."

"You know what I'd *just love* tonight?" said Kim. "A steak. We could clean off the barbecue, have a little picnic. Maybe your friend could buy some coleslaw, too. I mean, if he *owes* you . . ."

"A picnic," I said.

"A cookout. On the lawn. I need a break."

"From what?"

"From work," she said.

"I understand."

Kim leaned over and kissed my cheek. She left the room, then popped her head back in. "Tell your friend, if it's just for tonight, he can set up his tent in the yard. I mean, it's your house, too, and if you want a guest . . ."

"He hasn't asked to stay," I said. "But thank you."

"One more thing. If that's your money"—she pointed at the table—"could I maybe borrow twenty for some art supplies?"

"Actually, it's Lucas's money."

"I thought it was maybe a loan," said Kim. "I'm sorry."

"You need some art supplies."

"Yes, I really do."

"You're right. It's a loan."

Kim grinned.

The Lindgren selfishness.

Lucas marched into the kitchen with the groceries, acting as though he'd accomplished something grander than driving to a store and buying food. He set down the bulging bags on the table and said, "Prepare to feast." He took his time unpacking, setting out the cans and jars and bottles like exotic treasures that merited individual attention. The extent of his purchases unsettled me. Between the food, the twenties, and my St. Paul rent, I calculated my debt to Lucas as five hundred dollars, maybe even six.

"I couldn't choose between porterhouse and T-bone, so I got both," said Lucas. "The pork and the chicken I'll put in the freezer. Eat them when you like. The tea I suggest you store somewhere dry."

"No one here drinks tea. You didn't buy coffee?"

"Coffee, too. I bought it all."

Ricky set up the grill in the yard, and Kim spread a tablecloth out on the grass. Lucas mixed barbecue sauce in the kitchen. I offered to help him, but he wouldn't let me. "Patented secret recipe," he said. "If you like it, I'll give it to Kim."

"Kim doesn't cook."

"Doesn't want to, or doesn't know how?"

"Both."

Lucas opened a jar of molasses. "Maybe you'll teach her someday."

I showered, shaved, and brushed my teeth, then put on one of Bev's husband's best shirts, wanting to look as much as possible like the man of the house. By the time I finished washing up, everyone was sitting on the tablecloth, laughing and talking and drinking ale. Lucas must have seen some empties in our garbage can because he had bought a case of Ricky's brand. I had never seen Lucas drink before, and I wondered if he had just started. Or perhaps he'd been a drinker all along. Outside of Squad activities and church, I hadn't spent much time with him.

I opened a bottle of ale and sat down next to Kim, whose legs were spread a bit too wide, I thought, given how tight her jeans fit. I wondered how I could get her to move without calling more attention to them.

"Lucas was giving Ricky tips," Kim said. "Tips on organizing."

Lucas chuckled. " 'Dakota First.' I love it. Ricky has no idea what he's got there. Classic farm-states populism."

I looked at Ricky, whose face had turned red—from pride, I gathered, not embarrassment.

Lucas swallowed some ale, a hearty roadhouse chug. "That was my thesis topic in college: third-party movements. America's fringe."

I said, "I didn't know you went to college."

Lucas said, "I never mention it. Someone says he studied at Berkeley, everyone thinks he's some radical goofball. Especially if he went there in the sixties."

Kim looked impressed. "What was *that* like?" she said. "The sixties, I mean. You hear so much about them."

Lucas scored a point with me by taking Kim's dumb question seriously: "I wish I knew what happened then myself. America burned to the ground. We torched it. I say *we* because, for a while, I was in on the action. Draft cards, bras—we torched them all. Also, our minds. Our 'heads,' we called them." He chuckled. "That's how lost we were."

Ricky followed up with several comments relating sixties history to his own obsessions, but I was still trying to sort out Lucas's speech. Where did the Navy come in, the SEALs? I didn't want to put Lucas on the spot, but I needed this point cleared up.

"What did your Berkeley friends think when you enlisted?" I looked at Kim and Ricky and explained. "Lucas was a Navy diver."

Lucas scratched the salt-and-pepper chest hairs curling out through the V of his collar. His eyes were glazed. I wondered if he'd heard me.

Kim got up and stirred the coals.

Lucas said, "Weaver."

I looked at him.

"About the SEALs. I'm sorry. I exaggerated."

Ricky shook his head and laughed. "Everybody lies about his service. Sit in any barroom. Hell. If we'd had half the guys in Vietnam who've told me they got wounded there, we'd have won with human-wave attacks."

Lucas frowned, still facing me. "It's one of my problems," he said. "I embroider. I *was* in the SEALs, that's true, but only for a couple months. I joined on a dare from my dad, but then, when a buddy of mine got hurt in training, I claimed to be a homo, and they dropped me."

Ricky said, "Smart choice. I'll get the food," and hopped up and walked toward the porch. Kim followed him.

When they had gone, I said, "Lucas, tell me something. Where do you plan to stay tonight?"

He plucked a blade of grass and twirled it between two fingers and looked down. "I suppose that's what happens when men are honest. They wear out their invitations. So be it."

The heat of the barbecue grill was drawing out drops of sweat from my forehead. I drank some ale to cool down and said, "Your honesty I appreciate, Lucas. The problem is we just moved in. Everything's so disorganized."

"Believe me, I won't insist." Lucas snatched up more grass, this time by the roots. "If you want to retract the invitation, I understand. All I ask is you keep that thing from *Newsweek*. Maybe once you've read it again . . ."

"What do mean by 'retract'?"

"Ricky said I could camp by his van. Kim okayed it. She told me you had, too."

I heard the screen door creak open and saw Kim and Ricky over my shoulder. Ricky held a platter heaped with steaks and Kim had a pitcher of lemonade made fresh from Lucas's lemons. Picnic time.

"You won't even know I'm here," said Lucas. "Just for tonight. One night. So I won't have to go to some noisy campground and I can get some rest for once. I'm begging."

I sighed. "You don't have to beg."

"I am, though."

I looked away. I thought of Janet Cox. All the other Prozac victims.

Lucas said, "It's your decision."

Eighteen

THE MORNING AFTER THE BARBECUE, KIM'S NAUSEA WAS worse than ever. She woke up at seven, stumbled to the bathroom, and retched nonstop for half an hour. I had warned her at dinner not to overeat, but she had ignored me and taken second helpings. Also, despite my repeated dirty looks, she had drunk a bottle of ale. Now she was learning her lesson, I hoped. I sat up in bed with an old *Reader's Digest* ("I Battled Grizzlies—and Lived!"), listening to the ugly bathroom racket and feeling more and more annoyed. I couldn't concentrate. I couldn't read.

I threw off the covers, got up, and made coffee. Through the window above the kitchen sink I could see Luca's tent, a compact backpacking model, its flaps and mosquito netting zipped up tight. He had pitched it next to Ricky's van, not in the field, as he'd promised. The two of them had made friends in the night, staying up to talk politics long after Kim and I went to bed. Even with the bedroom window closed, I could hear them trading theories about the collapse of Russian communism.

Kim came into the kitchen looking awful. Her hair, which she usually brushed first thing, was all crushed down on top, a rat's nest. The corner of one eye was red where the force of her puking had ruptured a vessel. For breakfast, I served her a cup of strong black coffee and a slice of unbuttered wheat toast. She shivered picking the cup up and sloshed some coffee onto her T-shirt. I offered to get her a sweater from Bev's dresser, but she said she wouldn't wear her sister's clothes. I told her she was being ridiculous—anyone could see she was freezing.

"If you were a twin, you'd understand," Kim said. "You obviously aren't a twin."

The remark was uncalled for, I felt, as was one of the next things she said. She asked for some peanut butter for her toast (Lucas had bought a whole tub of extra-chunky) and I said, "You'll get sick again. Rich foods are what do it. You want to get sick again?"

Kim said, "How in the world would a *man* know what makes a pregnant woman sick?"

"You're being extremely unfair this morning."

I went to the cupboard for the peanut butter.

"Unfair," Kim said. "That's good. You sound like some kid on a playground: *It's unfair!*"

I pried the lid off the tub, jammed a spoon in, and set the tub on the table. "Eat. Throw up."

Kim's hand shot up and slapped her shoulder. "Something just bit me."

I rolled my eyes.

"Really. Something bit me. There's a bite." She pulled down her collar to show me. "A bedbug or something. A tick."

So she couldn't accuse me of not looking, I looked.

Nothing there.

She slapped her leg. "They're in my clothes!" she said.

Kim needed no more caffeine, I decided. I took away her coffee cup and dumped it out in the sink. As I set the cup in the drying rack, I saw the flap go up on Lucas's tent. He emerged headfirst, without a shirt, and stood and spread his arms and yawned.

Kim said, "How come you wouldn't make love to me last night?"

I turned around, sighing. "I told you. They'd hear us."

Kim plunged a finger into the peanut butter, then stuck it in her mouth and sucked. The sound was disgusting. So were her cheek movements. The finger came out shiny clean and she dipped it again, down to the knuckle. "I've figured it out. You loathe me," she said. "You think my body's icky, that it stinks. You're absolutely right. I'm fat and gross."

She scooped up a gob of peanut butter and flicked it at the wall.

I got a dishrag.

"A fat, gross pig," she said. Another gob flew.

I heard the back door open. Footsteps. I wiped the spots off the wall and quickly rinsed out the dishrag.

Lucas appeared in the doorway. "Good morning."

Kim nodded at him, then rose and left the room.

I hung the rag on a towel bar to dry. "Next time, knock," I said. "And wear some clothes."

Lucas said, "Is something wrong?"

I crossed the kitchen, going after Kim. "We're driving

into town," I said. "We have to see someone. A doctor. When we get back, I want you to be gone."

"You're the boss," said Lucas. "Just one thing, though."

I turned and glared at him. "What?"

"My timing chain. It snapped. My car won't start."

"You're lying," I said. "You haven't tried to start it."

"Ask Ricky," Lucas said. He lifted the coffeepot, eyed the liquid level, then poured himself all but the last ounce or two. "Anyway, why would I lie?"

"So you can stay."

Lucas laughed. "Stay here? Believe me, Weaver, it's not a pretty sight, seeing that little girl run you ragged. No— I'd like to leave as soon as possible. Get back out where a man can make a difference."

"I mean it," I said. "By the time we get back."

Lucas snapped me a Navy salute.

My mother the businesswoman hated women's libbers. Other people called them feminists, but she called them women's libbers. She hated them, she said, because they lied. They lied about biology.

I heard her discuss the subject once with the Cedar Lake Merchants Circle the only time they met at our house. She waved her celery stick as she spoke and swirled the ice cubes in her lime and tonic. The other merchants, all men, were drinking liquor—off-brand gin and vodka from the store—and hers was the clearest voice in the group. That was my mother's idea of entertaining: ply her guests with inexpensive alcohol, then start a conversation she could dominate.

"Take this business of periods," she said. From my spying post at the top of the stairs, I watched the other merchants nod and frown. "The women's libbers say periods don't matter, that they don't reduce women's effectiveness. Well, I have a female sales clerk—Lily—and when it's her time of the month, believe me, the customers know it. She crabs and whines. She counts people's change wrong and says it's their fault. Am I really supposed to pretend I don't *notice*? Pretend she's *fine and dandy*?"

The pharmacist said, "No, of course not."

"Or do I say, 'Lily, go home. Rest up,' and send her a little bouquet or some chocolates?"

The hardware-store owner said, "That's what I'd do."

"Anyone would," my mother said, "except for the women's libbers. *They* want poor Lily to *ignore* her pain. To deny it exists. But women *live* in pain."

I remembered all this as I watched Doctor Muntz draw blood from a vein in the crook of Kim's elbow. She tilted back her head and shut her eyes as the level rose in the syringe. When Doctor Muntz withdrew the needle and peeled the backing off a small, round bandage, she gave me a wasn't-I-brave look.

I melted.

I felt ashamed of my morning of annoyance and vowed to be more understanding from now on.

Doctor Muntz lectured Kim about nutrition and the importance of proper rest, then presented her with a jar of vitamins and sent us on our way. Putting on my seatbelt, I thought about Lucas's timing chain problem and how long such things can take to repair. I started the car and said, "How about a movie?"

Kim said, "Now?"

"Why not?"

"Because you hate them."

"Maybe I've changed," I said.

I was nervous as we stood in line for candy. Since join-
ing the Bryce Street Church of God, the only theater movie
I'd seen was a Disney cartoon, *The Little Mermaid,* on a
church-sponsored outing with the ten-and-unders. Halfway through the film I fled to the lobby, overcome by a
feeling of peril. I stayed there until the audience filed
out, laughing and grinning, with butter-smeared chins.
Though I've never been sure what spooked me that day,
I think it was the sight of all those children facing one
way in the dark.

It was not an isolated incident. Even before my baptism,
movies had been hard for me. I normally saw them stoned,
which heightened their effect. Whatever the movie's message was—that love conquers all, or that it doesn't; that
average people have hidden strengths which emerge only
in times of great stress; that achieving oneness with nature
heals all wounds—I would leave believing it and thinking
I should change my life accordingly. Eventually, it
dawned on me that I could not afford to switch philo-
sophies every Friday night. I stopped attending. If a movie
came out that interested me, I waited until the video appeared, then screened it at home, with the lights on.

I paid for Kim's Raisinets and told myself that this time
would be different. This time I would enjoy myself. Stay
calm.

I followed Kim down the aisle to some seats seven or
eight rows back from the screen. As I put my arm around
her and settled in for the coming attractions, I realized I
didn't know what we were seeing. I had given Kim the
money for the tickets—one of Lucas's crisp new twen-

ties—and said she could choose the movie. Now I couldn't remember what she'd picked.

I decided it didn't matter. The point was to be together, doing something fun. The point was to not go home until evening.

A half hour into the movie I knew I would be able to sit through it, but that Kim might not. Up on the screen, demolished human limbs spiraled end-over-end toward the camera, then dropped out of sight with a *splat*, drawing cheers from the mostly teenage audience. The killer's portable circular saw, shown to us through the eyeholes of his ski mask, reared up repeatedly, spitting hair and bone chips, and threw a shadow across the victims' faces. The moment the cute young female victims put up their hands to shield themselves, you knew the hands would soon be flying toward you. In one of the worst scenes, a college girl's class ring caused the revving chainsaw blade to seize, kicking it back in the killer's face and tearing out one of his eyes. The partial blinding enraged him and he finished off the murder with his fists.

The movie wasn't pleasant, but I could withstand the gore because of the anti-abortion films I'd seen: *The Silent Scream, Atrocity M.D., The Death of Baby Doe.* I had watched them in the chapel basement, a new one every month or so, sent to us from the clearinghouse in Georgia. The blood in those films was real, not ketchup. The organs arranged on the surgeons' steel trays were not just hunks of animal liver. This movie, though, was fantasy; a ketchup and pig-liver fantasy.

You did not have to take a stand because of it. You did not have to walk in the street with a sign.

You just ate Raisinets and let it happen.

I snugged my arm around Kim's shoulder and wondered

why she had chosen a movie she must have known would bother her. The noise of the killer's chainsaw made her cringe, and a few times she buried her face in my neck and didn't look up until the roaring stopped. I asked her if she would like to leave, but she said, "No, just hold me. I want to see what happens to the saw man."

She didn't have to wait; I could have told her. In that blasphemous horror-movie way, the saw man would be killed at the end and then rise again, like Jesus, in the sequel.

After the movie we stopped at Pizza Hut. Kim was good and had the salad bar. I had a small pepperoni and a Coke. We didn't talk much and Kim seemed tired. Leaving her lettuce untouched, she put Italian olives in her mouth, spat out the pits in her palm, and arranged them on her napkin in a circle resembling a tiny Stonehenge. When I got bored watching her do this, I asked her what she thought about the movie.

"I've seen it before," she said.

"When?"

"With Loring."

The name didn't register.

Then it did: the father.

"You didn't know the ending, though," I said.

"Loring made us leave. He said he couldn't bear the violence."

I sucked up the last of the Coke through a straw and looked at my empty plate, the pizza crusts. I felt I was being condemned for something. Perhaps I should have left the horror movie out of principle.

Kim let me off the hook a moment later, "We're talking about the same Loring, of course, who pissed on my walls and destroyed my apartment. Which just goes to show you . . ."

"You never can tell."

Kim put a hand to her lips and ejected another pit. "You're right, you can't. The best you can do is have faith, I guess."

I nodded, encouraged. "Faith is the answer."

Kim said, "I meant in people, not God. God you don't have to have faith in: he's perfect."

I considered Kim's idea as we drove home, then thought about it again when we arrived. Because Lucas's tent was still pitched in the yard, and I did not know what to do about him.

Nineteen

THAT NIGHT A COYOTE HOWLED BEHIND THE HOUSE. OR MAYBE
it was an ordinary dog—some family's black lab running
loose on the prairie, surviving on voles and field mice.
Pets that return to the wild, they say, are fiercer than the
creatures who grow up there. Whatever the thing that
howled was, though, it scared me. Suddenly, all North
Dakota was a bubble, a huge soundproof membrane sealing in our lives.

I was alone on the sofa in the living room, flipping
through old local newspapers. Kim had gone to bed, and
Lucas and Ricky were in the garage, working on Lucas's
engine. The timing-chain problem was real, apparently.
Ricky had even shown me the part. When I asked him

how long the repairs would take, he said another hour, maybe two. That had been three hours ago. I decided to check again in fifteen minutes. If necessary, I'd stay awake all night.

The newspapers I was reading depressed me. "Scout Troop Short of Funds for D.C. Trip." "Drought Continues." "Fargo Gas War." The crimes in the police blotter were all either DUIs or Failures to Appear, and some were combinations of both. Back in Wisconsin, growing up, I myself had been caught driving drunk once, but to my credit, I had appeared. My mother the businesswoman went with me. In a sort of black mourning dress bought for the occasion, she asked the judge to throw the book at me. The drunken son of a liquor-store owner, whose father had died in a drunken hunting accident, deserved to be treated more harshly, she said, than the average citizen. Realizing what I was up against at home, the judge let me off with a minor fine.

When the coyote or dog started howling, I put down the papers and went to check on Kim. She was lying on her stomach, naked. Her right arm, still wearing the blood-test bandage, was twisted around behind her back in a way that made it look broken or dislocated. I heard a car in the driveway, saw headlights, and softly closed the bedroom door.

I went to the front door to answer a knock.

It was Chuck, with flowers.

I couldn't help being angry with him, bouquet or no bouquet. "Your daughter's asleep," I said. "She's exhausted, so unless it's important . . ."

Chuck said, "Let her rest. I'd like you to give her these roses, please." He pushed the bouquet at my nose, as if to assure me the roses weren't plastic.

"Fine," I said. "I'll pass them on."

Chuck said, "There's a bank slip in the card. I opened the account in her name—Kim's—and deposited a thousand dollars. I would have deposited more, but Dixie . . ."

"Yes?

Chuck rubbed his hand across his stubbly chin. "My wife is not sympathetic. She's made plans. If her daughter can't plan her own life, my wife feels, that's her daughter's fault."

"I see."

Chuck looked straight at me. "I see my wife's point."

"That's your privilege, sir."

"Except I believe that everything's unplanned, so how can I be angry? Agnes—Kim—and Bev weren't exactly planned. Neither was Ricky, as I remember. I'm certain some people plan their children—or at least they tell themselves they do, when really it's just nature pulling them—but to me that's, well, foreign. And sad. It's like when a person hires outsiders to decorate his house. It saddens me."

I saw him look down at the roses in his hand. A lock of incredibly fine white hair fell across his forehead, and suddenly I was aware of Chuck's age. Old, and getting older as we spoke.

"This house, as you may know," he said, "is mine. Live here as long you want and pay me when you're able. My Bev has left her husband, met some man. Some Alaska man, with two grown kids. Her husband, Mike, I hear, is in Kuwait. Only God knows why."

"I'm sorry to hear that." I meant it.

"I don't understand Bev's arrangement," Chuck said, "but then I'm unclear on your arrangement, too." He pushed back the lock of hair and looked away. "Under-standing is not required, though. Love is. Do you love my daughter?"

"Yes."

"Then we have something in common."

Chuck handed me the flowers. He went down the porch steps, then turned at the bottom. "By the way," he said, "we're leaving. Tomorrow morning, for Tucson, Arizona. We may be back, but I don't know when, and it probably won't be soon. The truth is we hate the winters here. We freeze. In the summers, we hate the bugs. We hate it all."

His forehead wrinkled up, relaxed, then wrinkled up again. He rested his hands on the hips of his slacks, hook-ing his thumbs in the pockets. On his wrist, I could see the glowing green numbers of the chronograph.

"Across the road," he said, "what crop is that? The one you wake up and look at every morning."

I stalled. "The field behind you?"

Chuck nodded. "Here's a hint: it isn't corn."

It was too dark to see across the road, but the crop would have been as mysterious to me at noon on a sunny day.

"I honestly don't know," I said. "I haven't paid atten-tion."

Chuck shook his head. "Don't worry, my own kids don't know either. And neither will their kids, I'm sure. It's finished here. You know that marijuana Ricky grew?"

I waited.

"That was my idea," said Chuck. "Plants are plants, in my book. Whatever grows, deserves to. Now, that project's bust like all the others. . . ."

I couldn't let him leave like this. "You and Kim should say good-bye. Wait here. I'll wake her up."

Chuck ignored me. Crossing the yard to the driveway, he reminded me of an injured football player trying to show the crowd he's okay: square-set shoulders, jutting chin, legs lifted unnecessarily high. Once in his car, behind the windshield, he gave a courteous wave and backed down the driveway and onto the road, failing to turn on his headlights until he had driven a quarter mile or so.

In the kitchen, I stripped the wrapping off the roses, then found an empty jelly jar and poured in a couple of inches of water. The small pink envelope clipped to the wrapping wasn't properly sealed. I slipped the card out.

Dear Kim,
I'm sure you've made the right decision. Sorry I'm too old to help you with it. You'll get over that, though. We always do.

Love,
Dixie

I arranged the bouquet in the jar and set the jar in the middle of the table. I laid the bank deposit slip beside it. I replaced the card in the envelope.

"Nice roses."

I turned and saw Lucas, shirtless again. His hands and wrists were black from grease, coated to the elbows. He was drinking one of Ricky's ales.

I squared my shoulders. "Finished with the car?"

"Almost. That kid's a whiz. Scatterbrained, yeah, but that can be corrected. . . ." He set down his ale and crossed toward the refrigerator. He reached for the door.

"Let me," I said. "Your hands."

190

"Sorry. Forgot. Forgot that you're the cleaning woman here."

I opened the refrigerator door. Ignore him—let it go. He's leaving soon.

"Get out that leftover steak," said Lucas, standing over my shoulder. "And some bread. Ricky and I want a sandwich for the road."

"Where's Ricky going?"

"None of your beeswax. Camping trip. He's restless."

I found the bread on the middle shelf, but didn't see the steak.

Lucas prompted me. "In the meat compartment."

I opened the plastic drawer. The steak was there.

"Shit—she didn't wrap it. *Fuck!*" Lucas shoved me aside, reached down, and grabbed the meat drawer, yanking it off its rails. He slammed it down on the countertop and lifted the steak out. He held it to his nose. "This is spoiled," he said. "You smell that?"

"Lucas, calm down."

"It's rotten meat. She wrecked it." He dropped the steak on the counter, then wiped his hands down his abdomen, leaving black parallel tracks of grease. "I'm telling you, Weaver, you can *have* that girl."

"That's all I want."

He picked up his ale bottle, chugged it, wiped his mouth with the back of his hand. Soon, his entire body would be black. "I feel for you," he said. "I really do. This is an upside-down world in this house, and you are on the bottom."

"That's my problem."

"Except that you're setting a precedent here. Private lives breed public laws. If the laws of this house were the laws of the land, I'd emigrate to China."

"Go ahead."

"Maybe I will someday." He cut his eyes at the roses. "Those from you? Those fragrant blossoms?"

"Yes." Taking responsibility.

"Flowers for the mother," Lucas said. "The mother-to-be. Is that the idea?"

"That's the idea."

"Then maybe I ought to tell you a secret. It might affect your gift-giving."

Terror, with me, begins in the mouth. A chemical dryness, as if I've licked a penny. Then my legs. They seem to disappear. I'm standing, but I don't know how.

"It's under the sink," said Lucas. "In a bucket. I found it while you were gone. You want to see it?"

Some moisture returned to my mouth. A trickle. I had expected something much worse. Worse than a physical object in a bucket.

Lucas crouched and opened the cabinet. He reached inside and came out with something red: a hot-water bottle. He set it on the counter. He reached in again and extracted a tube, a white plastic tube about two feet long. He laid it next to the bottle. An exhibit.

"Now, that," he said, standing back up, "is a douche bag."

"You lied. You're still on those pills," I said.

He opened the tap and filled the bottle, then inserted the tube in the neck. He turned and faced me, holding the tube in one hand, the bottle in the other. He kept the mouth of the tube above the bottle. "Douche bag," he repeated.

"Also known as a hot-water bottle."

"Or an enema kit. But that's not why she has this thing.

That's not why it smells of Lysol. You know why it smells of Lysol inside?'' He lifted the bag to the level of his head, keeping the tube-end pinched between two fingers. "Or do I need to fill you in on traditional female folk cures?''

I understood him now. And he was wrong. We'd been to the doctor today, and Kim was fine. Her child was safe inside her. Lucas didn't know that, though, and I saw no reason to tell him. I decided to let him run with this. Get tired. Play his scene and leave.

"I'm sorry, Weaver. Because maybe this thing worked, or maybe not. Doesn't matter legally. What matters is intent. Intent to kill. The greatest slaughter since Hitler built his ovens—and none of us are safe.''

Lucas's face was flushed from neck to hairline. Once again, I felt sorry for him.

"That's all very shocking,'' I said. "Go fix your car.''

"Excuse me, those roses look a bit dried out.''

He pointed the tube and raised the bag, holding it as high as he could reach. Water squirted everywhere, a pressurized arcing stream that hit the farthest wall of the kitchen, then the stovetop, then the microwave. He sprayed the room machine-gun style, shooting from the hip, then, as the water ran out, trained a last feeble burst on the roses. I just stood there, watching him. I wanted to fix this image in my mind. Burn out my last trace of pity for this man.

"That,'' he said, tossing the bottle in the sink, "is a dangerous murder weapon.'' He laughed. "You catch her on the john with that, you'll see what I mean.''

"You're insane.''

"Telepathic, too. I know what that girl is thinking. Planning. You're the only one too blind to see it.''

He ran a hand through his hair, then rubbed his throat,

filling up with black. He spat in the sink, then turned and left. I followed him to the door and watched him cross the lawn to the garage. A few minutes later, Ricky pulled the car out. Lucas got in. They drove away together. I went to the kitchen and mopped up the mess.

I hid the hot-water bottle on a shelf you have to stand on a stool to reach.

Twenty

KIM AND I WENT TO CHURCH IN THE MORNING. I DIDN'T FORCE her—it was her idea. It came to her in her studio, she said, the moment she sat down to work on her cards. Just a vague impulse, she said. A notion. This worried me a little. I wondered if Kim had done something, thought something, that had made her feel guilty, in need of absolution. Then I decided not to question something I had wanted all along for her. I kissed Kim on the cheek and quickly put on my good black penny-loafers, hurrying so that she would not have time to lose her inspiration.

The church was a white pioneer-style Lutheran chapel ten miles away in Mapleton. The chapel stood in a hayfield, all alone, as if it had been set down by a tornado. Kim said she'd always admired the building, its tidy architecture, and had wondered what it looked like on the inside. And though I would have preferred a sect with a sounder scriptural grounding (the Lutherans, like the Episcopalians, had thrown out the Holy Bible in the sixties), I knew that first steps are often small steps. Mimicking an older couple walking up ahead of us, I slid my arm around Kim's waist and guided her through the tall front door.

I sensed a certain resistance in Kim once we got inside, and though I knew it was perfectly natural, her shyness broke my heart. That anyone should fear God's house, his people. I whispered, "It's okay, we'll sit back here," and pointed to a pew beneath the choir. Experience had taught me that sitting so far to the rear would place us in the company of latecomers, other visitors, and disgraced or unpopular congregants, but maybe that was as it should be. Kim and I were sinners, after all, and to sit at the front with the white-haired elders and their blue-haired wives would have been presumptuous.

The service was scheduled to start at ten, but the organ was silent until a quarter after. I read the mimeoed program as we waited, leaving Kim alone with her thoughts—whatever they might have been that morning.

The title of the sermon, "One Planet, One Peace," discouraged me: it smacked of humanism. It made me think of rock concerts for hunger—of long-haired millionaire singers and guitarists lecturing stadium crowds about self-sacrifice. It made me think of the liberal Catholic bishops Pastor Spannring liked to call "priestniks." I replaced the program in its rack. I wondered what Lucas was up to right now—if he and Ricky were also in church. I suspected they were not.

I said a silent prayer for Ricky. He had made a poor

choice in going off with Lucas, but so had I, at one time.
I prayed for his safety. His soul. I prayed he would come
back soon to Bev's house. Perhaps if I'd paid more attention to him, he would not have left. Two days ago, during
one of his tirades, I had asked him to lower his voice. A
mistake.

When I finished praying, I laid my hand on Kim's knee
and smiled at her. She lowered her eyes—still shy, it
seemed—and fiddled with the rosebud pinned to the front
of her dress. The dress had come with a belt when I bought
it, but I noticed Kim was not wearing the belt, perhaps
because it no longer fit. She had gained some weight that
week. A pound or two. She said her breasts felt tender. Everything was progressing naturally. Everything on
course.

I didn't pay much attention to the service. I focused on
Kim's reactions to it. For the first few minutes she stood
there straight and stiff, mouthing the hymns without
really singing them. She squinted during the Bible read-
ings, as though she were trying to see the words in print.
Once or twice, she stroked her throat and very inconspic-
uously cleared it. Then something happened: a woman
sat down next to me, a mother with a baby in her arms.

Actually, the woman was a girl, probably only seven-
teen or eighteen, with choppy colorless hair and rugged
bands of acne across her cheeks and forehead. Her blouse
and skirt were Salvation Army specials—they appeared
to be decades apart in style and material. Her eyes looked
almost terminally tired, with blue scooped-out hollows
beneath them, and she and the baby seemed to share a
cold. Their noses were red and runny and chapped. They
sat down just as the sermon started, just as the pastor was
opening his mouth. Then the mother sneezed.

Her sneezes were loud and ridiculously messy. Mucus covered her lips and chin and spotted the front of her blouse. Her hands were full with the baby, though, and when she tried to free an arm to wipe the stuff away, the baby spat out its pacifier. The mother leaned forward to catch it and missed. The pacifier rolled under the pew.

Kim said, "Let me help you. Here."

I saw the mother's eyes light up with thanks as Kim reached across in front of me and gathered in the cranky baby. Supporting the head in the proper way, she bounced the baby up and down and made a shushing sound. The baby howled. She dabbed the little nose clean with her finger. The baby bawled louder, waving its fists. I looked over at the mother, who was occupied with licking a tissue and wiping at her blouse-front. She said, "I'll just be a minute," and turned, heading toward the aisle.

I whispered, "Where are you going?"

"Ladies' room."

I looked back at Kim. The baby wouldn't quit. I remembered the pacifier on the floor. I leaned way down; I couldn't find it. The baby's screams were filling up the chapel, putting its acoustics to the test. Two old women with matching hairnets who were sitting directly in front of us swiveled their heads around, scowled. I scowled back at them. I felt Kim jabbing my side with her elbow.

"What?" I said.

"You take it."

"She's coming right back," I whispered.

"*Take* the thing."

The baby kicked and squirmed as it was passed. I didn't know how to hold it. I knew about the head, but not the legs. The legs were out of control. I gripped the ankles. One hand around both ankles. But that seemed wrong—

too brutal. I let go. There seemed to be no way to hold the baby without either crushing it or dropping it on the floor.

"Sir?"

I looked to the side: a boy in uniform. An altar boy or something.

"Would you like to sit out in the lobby?" he whispered.

Over his shoulder I saw the mother. She pushed in past him. Her blouse was water-stained. She had the pacifier in her hand. She tucked the nub in the baby's mouth, then lifted him out of my hands and said, "Thank you. This is the last time I bring the brat. I've had it."

I looked back at Kim, who was facing the pastor. Her knees and ankles were pressed tight together; her jawline was ruler-straight. The pastor read a verse from Solomon that I had never heard spoken in a church: "Take us the foxes, the little foxes, that spoil the vines: for our vines have tender grapes." I had missed his lead-up, though, and I had no idea what his point was.

I glanced at the baby. Asleep now. From monster to angel in less than a minute.

Soon, it was time for communion. The people in back were meant to go first. I stayed put, of course, because I was not a Lutheran, but Kim did not know the rules, apparently. When the mother stood, Kim stood. They filed down together. I watched her kneel before the black-robed pastor, eat of the body, drink the blood.

In the lobby, after the service, Kim said she wanted coffee and doughnuts.

"Let's just go," I said. "We can have breakfast at home."

Kim said, "What's wrong? You didn't like the service?"

"Nothing's wrong. It was fine. Go eat your doughnut."

Kim joined the line by the serving table; I hung back

by the coatracks. Something *was* wrong. Those words Kim had used of the baby: "That *thing*." The way she had flubbed up holding it, as I had. And indeed the woman's baby *was* a "thing." Kicking, resistant. An alien bundle. I thought of the Superman legend: an infant is placed in a spacecraft and launched from a dying planet. A farmer finds the spacecraft in a field. As the boy grows older, the farmer is shocked by its strange, unearthly powers—he catches it tossing his cows around, lifting tractors over its head.

Perhaps it was always that way with children. Perhaps they never seemed like yours.

What if the baby growing inside her also felt like a "thing" to Kim?

I watched her sip coffee and chat with the pastor. Their bodies were turned so I couldn't see their faces. I wondered what Kim had to say to the man. Maybe she was just praising his sermon. Maybe they were discussing the weather.

Or maybe something was troubling her.

Twenty-one

EXCEPT FOR A PHONE CALL FROM RICKY IN WHICH HE TOLD KIM he was camping with Lucas and that she shouldn't worry, nothing much happened on Monday. It passed. Kim and I had sex once—still no penetration, just our hands—but it was not a memorable event for me. I did it to please her, and I suspect I failed. Monday was forgettable.

Tuesday, though, I will always remember.

A prayer of mine was granted after breakfast: Kim sold one of her card designs (a boy on a beach saying, "Crappy surfday, dude!") to what she called an "important small company" based in New York City. The telephone rang, I picked it up, an excited soprano male voice asked for Kim, and ten minutes later she was telling me that not only had she earned five hundred dollars, but that the company wanted more cards: one for each major holiday including Halloween, using the same teenage character.

Instead of being elated by the news, Kim looked stern and worried. She sat at her desk and stared at her materials. I asked her what was wrong.

"I did that card a year ago," she said. "I don't even know where it came from now. What if I can't get back to that?"

"That what?"

"That mood. That attitude." She rested her head in her hands and rubbed her temples with her fingertips. I moved in to rub them for her. I felt the problem-vein throb. Eventually, Kim relaxed and said, "I really can't complain. It's what I always wanted: one small break."

I left Kim's studio feeling good and bad—good for her, bad for me. I had to earn some money. I had to start contributing. My mother's check was due any day, and there was the thousand dollars from Chuck, but none of that was mine. It didn't count. In the Walquist-Lindgren household ledger, the number under my name was still zero.

I walked the length of the driveway, thinking, scuffing my toes in the gravel. Maybe Sanipure would take me back. For only four hundred dollars, I could open my own distributorship, and though I would have to go door-to-door at first ("I'd like to speak with the lady of the house about an amazing beauty revolution"), it wouldn't take long, if I applied myself, to rope in people under me and build the pyramid. The reasons I had failed before—misgivings concerning product quality, shyness, plain old sloth—did not have to get in my way this time around. This time, I would bear in mind the words of Conrad Burns, repulsive human being but extraordinary salesman: "Sanipure means what we make it mean, so we must make it mean everything to everyone we meet."

Just dial a toll-free number, send a check, and I would be back in business.

Problem solved.

But I did not make the phone call right away. I decided to call the next morning, when I was in a more positive mood. Today, I wanted to buy a gift for Kim. Something to help her celebrate her sale—a bottle of champagne, perhaps. Not a big one, a small one. A split. Just enough for a single toast, harmless to the baby. The gift would show Kim that I was behind her and prove I did not begrudge her her success. Two small glasses of good champagne, as in 1 Timothy 23: *Drink no longer water, but use a little wine for thy stomach's sake and thine often infirmities.*

I found Kim still in her studio, sketching in charcoal on a large white pad. I wanted to surprise her with the wine, so I lied about where I was going.

"I'm running to town for a newspaper. Anything you need? A *Vogue* or a *Vanity Fair* or something?"

She drew a small black curve, an eyebrow for her irreverent teen surfer. "Just peace and quiet," she said.

I knew the car would be hot inside after baking in the sun all morning, so I took two cold bottles of ale along. I opened one and turned on the radio. The resolute voice of the Reverend Armand Dale counseling a troubled caller.

"Ernie, your problem's not poverty, it's doubt. Fact is, from what you've told me, you're not even all that poor. You have an apartment, a VCR, a car—"

"Sears *repossessed* the VCR."

"I'm sorry, Ernie, I still say doubt. You doubt the Lord's

abilities. Not only can He return your VCR, He can teach you how to live *without* one. Why don't you pray not to need this device?"

"I've never heard of praying not to have things."

"You're hearing it today, my friend."

The caller hung up in a huff. I checked my speedometer: eighty. I slowed down. When I parked in front of the liquor store, both ale bottles were empty, but I did not feel the least bit drunk. I reached to turn off the radio and heard Reverend Dale say—to me, to no one else—"Fargo, North Dakota, prepare to hear God's word. At eleven A.M. this Thursday, I will be taping my cable show, 'Positions,' at the Roosevelt Street Ecumenical Center. Admission is free, and I hope to see you there."

I promised myself I'd attend—with Kim, if I could persuade her to go.

I went to the back of the liquor store and opened the glass-doored wine case. My mother the businesswoman would have laughed out loud at the selection. There wasn't a single true champagne, only cheap Spumantes and California sparkling wines. I considered having a word with the clerk, but I could see he was not a wine type, so I picked the prettiest label. I also bought a pint of cherry schnapps. Something to have in the house. A sleeping aid. To check the schnapps's quality, I downed a quick ounce or two on the sidewalk, then screwed the cap on extra-tight.

Across the street I saw a bar whose window advertised buffalo burgers. Standing in a field behind the bar was a waterslide. The enormous spiraling fiberglass tubes rose up out of the prairie flatness like a section of Hell's own plumbing. Little kids and teenagers climbed the open staircase bolted to the tubes. When they reached the top, they belly flopped onto yellow mats and disappeared into the mouth of the monster. I could not see the pool where they splashed down, but I could hear the screams. The girls screamed loudest, as girls always do. I wondered why that was.

Instead of going straight home to Kim and perhaps interrupting her work again, I decided to try a buffalo burger. I sat at the bar and watched an old man cook it. The heat from the grill was intense; I ordered a beer, a mug of draft. The old man flopped the burger on a bun and set it in front of me on a paper plate. I noticed a Fargo newspaper lying on the bar. The old man said, "It's yesterday's," but I had fallen behind, so I grabbed it.

Centered up high on the front page I saw them: Lucas and Ricky.

I set down my burger.

In the photograph, which was printed in color (the editors must have suspected they had a prize-winning image on their hands), Lucas and Ricky stood side by side on the steps of the North Dakota capitol, joined at the neck by a U-shaped bike lock. They were soaked from head to toe in what the photo's caption said was calves' blood. They must have poured a few gallons on themselves: the blackish red liquid spilled down the staircase in sheets and ribbons, a waterfall of gore. The white marble steps and columns of the capitol lent the scene an ancient feel, as if it were set in Rome or Carthage, not modern-day Bismarck. The faces seemed ancient, too. Historical. Instead of hiding the two men's features, the blood had heightened them, fixed them into masks. Lucas grinning, Ricky grim and pinched.

"Right-to-lifers Outraged over Veto."

I asked for a shot of vodka and another beer. The old

man brought the drinks. He nodded at the paper, then at my uneaten burger, and said, "Sort of thing that makes you vegetarian."

I worked on the shot and beer as I read. According to the article, which mostly dealt with a speech by the governor ("The bill's undoubted merits were somewhat outweighed by its flaws"), state police had arrested the protesters and later released them on their own recognizance. That word jumped out at me: *recognizance*. I wondered what it meant exactly and if Lucas had ever had any. Reading on, I was not surprised to learn that Richard Charles Lindgren already had a criminal record: possession of marijuana, petty theft. Lucas Boone, on the other hand, was a "decorated Navy veteran and leading pro-life activist." It was just like him, I thought, to get those words in: *decorated*, *leading*. And to persuade the reporter not to double-check them.

I shut my eyes and rubbed them with my fists, but red is a color that sticks in your mind. There were pink man-shaped ghosts on the backbar mirror when I looked back up. There also were two new drinks in front of me—on the house, apparently. I downed the shot, but saved the beer, then walked to a pay phone next to the pool table.

"It's me," I said. "Hello? It's Weaver, Kim."

The bubble was tightly sealed around me, and I was not sure my voice was getting through.

Kim said, "Where are you? You have to come home."

"Buffalo bar. Eating buffalo burgers. There's this gigantic waterslide out back. . . ."

"You've been riding waterslides?"

"No. Been drinking. Little wine. Here's the thing, though: Want to see a movie? How about it? Take our minds off things."

When Kim did not respond, I passed my hand in front of my mouth to clear away the bubble film. Then I had the oddest memory, one that I later described to my mother and found out wasn't real. I was a child in an oxygen tent. My breathing echoed inside the plastic walls. The monitor next to my head showed wavy lines as blurry doctors adjusted its dials. My father's nose was pressed against the tent.

"Weaver, listen to me." Kim's voice had dropped to a whisper. "They're back. They got here an hour ago, and . . . Excuse me?"

I heard Lucas's voice in the background. Then it was in the foreground, in my ear. "Brother, did you miss the party! Costumes, speeches, feats of strength—a genuine gala occasion."

"Give the phone to Kim."

"Gave us quite a beating," Lucas said. "State policeman did. Ricky here looks like a—I don't know—a Bozo clown. Hey, you ever notice that? How a clown's face is just a normal man's face, only all bruised up and swollen?"

"I have to talk to Kim," I said. "Where is she?"

"Agnes is busy," Lucas said. "She's serving the boys their tea. We're having a proper high tea here. Welcome home the troops."

"If you so much as touch her—"

"Why should I touch her? All I want is one nice cup of tea the way my dear wife used to make it. That cunt."

I said I would be there and hung up the phone. The old man set down the glass he was drying when I turned around. My expression must have been crazy; he looked frightened. I opened my wallet and tossed a few bills on the bar.

The old man said, "Oh, no, you're not."

At first, I thought he meant he wasn't going to let me pay. Then I saw my car keys in his hand. I must have left them sitting on the bar.

The old man said, "You're drunk, my boy. You get in a wreck, I'm responsible. State law. I had a guy sue me last year. I learned my lesson." He dropped my keys in the cash drawer of his register and slammed it shut. "Black coffee time."

"I'm not going to sue you. I promise."

"Kid, you have no idea what you'll do."

"I mean it. I have to leave *now*. My girlfriend's in trouble."

"Yes, she is. Has a drunk for a boyfriend."

I shrugged and sat down on my stool. When the old man brought my coffee, I grabbed both his wrists and yanked him down and toward me. His head banged the bar, upsetting the coffee cup and rattling some wine-glasses hanging from a ceiling rack. The old man yelled, "You *fuck!*" as I twisted my fist in his fine gray hair and demanded my car keys back. "You shit!" he screamed. I let go of his hair to see what he would do. He didn't move, just drooled and shook and bled. I crossed behind the bar and punched a button on the register. I pocketed my keys. I noticed a paring knife on the drainboard—the kind with a short, curled blade. I took it with me.

As I was walking out the front door, I heard a sharp, metallic noise behind me, and I felt sure the old man had pulled a pistol. I didn't turn to look, just prayed that the gun, if there was a gun, would jam. And perhaps that's exactly what happened. Perhaps my prayer was answered. Perhaps an invisible hand reached down and saved me.

Twenty-two

IN TIPPY HIGH HEELS AND WEARING A GOWN SHE MUST HAVE found in her twin sister's closet, Kim met me at the door and said, "Come in." Her freshly brushed hair was pinned up tight in back and her cheeks were smudged with bubble-gum-pink rouge. Her smile was hard, with high, taut corners, and I guessed she had either just got done crying or was about to start. She looked disastrous. I reached for her elbow, to soothe her; she pulled back. Then, in a whisper, with cautious sidelong eyes: "Weaver, play along. Just do it. He promised me he'd leave if I don't fight him."

She ushered me into the living room, then veered off toward the kitchen. I could see where I was meant to sit: in the lawn chair from the porch, which had been placed in the center of the room so as to form a circle with the sofa and rocker-recliner. Ricky, smoking a joint, was on the sofa. Lucas had the recliner. Its back was set to the first degree of tilt, and Lucas had his feet up on the matching ottoman. The knife I had seen in his glove compartment once, a hunting knife with a saw-toothed back, lay across his lap.

The knife blade was rusty; it didn't gleam.

It didn't have to gleam.

Lucas nodded as I took my seat. His forehead was swollen just under the hairline, and his right eye looked puffy and tender, but he still had a human face, of sorts. Ricky, though, was Bozo. Worse than Bozo. An attempt had been made to cover his bruises with flesh-tone foundation makeup, but because the skin itself was not even vaguely flesh-tone but a bluish fruity color, the effect was hideous. His hands were bandaged in white cloth tape, and they rested on the sofa at his sides, palms up and slightly curled, not moving. The joint in his lips was smoking itself; every few seconds, I heard a sucking sound, saw the tip glow orange, then watched the smoke pour out his one good nostril. The other nostril was flat, caved in, as was the ear on the same side.

Lucas eased his chair back another notch or two. "The preparation and serving of tea is a dying art," he said. "I expect it will be revived once the Japanese take over— 1995 or so, I'm guessing—but for the moment, consider it dead. Dead as the Edsel, to quote the TV. That's their cliché for defunctness: the Edsel."

Lucas seemed to expect a response, and I knew it would not come from Ricky.

"The Edsel. That was a car," I said. I heard the tea kettle whistle in the kitchen and thought of the paring knife stashed in my pants pocket. I wondered if its outline was detectable, but I didn't dare look down to check.

"To someone of your generation," Lucas said, "the Edsel's not even a car, it's a reference. That's how the media steals your mind. They take this car you've never even seen; they use it over and over as a symbol, really drum it into you; then make you feel smart, like a really clued-in cat, every time you catch their . . ."

He seemed to lose his concentration then. I sensed he had made the speech many times before and was bored with it. His gaze wandered over to Ricky. "One courageous kid," he said. "Sadly, he's temporarily deaf. Those cops clapped his ears like you would not believe."

I said, "He needs a doctor."

"He resisted. He deserved it," Lucas said.

"You both need a doctor. Let me call one."

Lucas ran a ragged, dirty thumbnail along the notched back of his knife. "I do hope she brings the pot to the kettle, not the kettle to the pot. Temperature, as I used to tell my wife, is everything with tea."

"Why don't you let me help her?" I made a tentative move to stand up.

Lucas glared at me. "Stay put. It isn't your job—it's hers. I'll go when she's done it, not before."

"Go where?"

"Wherever the cause needs a boost. Wherever the battle's pitched. I'm thinking Idaho."

Kim emerged from the kitchen carrying the tea tray. It seemed she had been given meticulous instructions. The teapot was swathed in a yellow dish towel. The cups were upside down on saucers. Crustless white-bread sandwiches the size and shape of cigarette packs were stacked on a plate, topped by parsley sprigs. She crossed the room to the middle of our circle and set the tray on the coffee table. She lifted the lid off the pot and said, "How strong do you like it?"

She was asking Lucas.

"Let it brew," he said. He looked at me. "This is Earl Grey. It needs to steep. Very delicate flavor, very British."

Ricky coughed; I turned my head. The end of the joint had dropped onto his lap. He brushed it onto the floor and stamped it out.

"Fuck them all," he said. His eyelids fluttered shut and his curled-up fingers straightened out. Only the rise and fall of his chest indicated he was still alive.

I saw Kim bend over, preparing to pour. The way the chairs were arranged, there was no way to flash her a signal I could be certain Lucas wouldn't see, or for her to flash me one. I imagined that in our hearts and souls Kim and I were huddled close together, waiting out the storm, but that is one of those things you can't know. You can discuss it afterward, but there is no guarantee you'll get truth. Indeed, I have already lied by saying my thoughts were with Kim as she poured. Really, I was concerned with the tea. I was hoping Kim had brewed it properly and Lucas would find it to his satisfaction.

She turned to him. "Milk and sugar?"

"There wasn't a lemon?" he said.

"I'm sorry."

"Black then. Milk makes mucus. I don't need that."

Kim handed him his cup and saucer. Then she passed me mine. It was our chance to look at each other, but Kim's hand was trembling, rattling the cup, and I think she was just too frightened to make eye contact.

Lucas said, "You didn't take his order. Maybe your boyfriend wants sugar in his."

I quickly sipped my tea. "It's fine," I said.

"Do it over. Ask him," Lucas said to Kim. "For crying out loud, girl, I'm trying to *teach* you. Don't you want to *learn?*"

Kim did not move or speak. She stood there, facing Ricky, whose eyes were the half-open watery eyes of a dog that seems to be sleeping but might not be. Perhaps she was waiting for her older brother suddenly to rouse himself, leap into action. Or for me to do that. Lucas's hands were on his cup and saucer, and it would have been the optimum moment to spring at him with the paring knife. Not a good moment, just the best one. No matter how much of a jump I got on him, Lucas would probably stab me first, then stab Kim, and maybe Ricky, and so on and so on across the country, all the way to Idaho. Assuming the whole thing was not a joke. In a way, I believed it *was* a joke, but also that if I tried to cut it short, Lucas would turn it into something else.

So I did not attack. And maybe Kim was not waiting for me to. Maybe she was waiting for herself to.

In any case, after a pause, she said, "I'm sorry. Milk or sugar, Weaver?"

She looked me in the eye this time, but I had no idea whom she was seeing. By the anger and pain and loathing in her face, I would have hated to think it was me.

I said, "Neither. Thank you."

Kim said, "You're welcome," and turned to Lucas. "Since I don't think my brother wants any tea, if he can even swallow anymore, I'd like to go to bed now and do the dishes later."

Lucas set his teacup on the floor. The color of his face had grown unstable, turning from red to white to red every few seconds—a lava-lamp effect. "Come here," he said. "Come over here."

Kim stood there.

"Come here and unbutton that dress," said Lucas. "I want to feel that belly. See how the little angel is progressing."

My hand crept down to my pocket. I touched the handle of the paring knife. Such a ridiculous weapon.

Lucas said to Kim, "I fathered two children myself, you know. A boy and a girl, and they're both just darling. I wish I had snapshots on me. I don't. Their mother took them. The snapshots *and* the kids."

Ricky started snoring—difficult-sounding one-nostril snores. Outside, the wind was picking up, bowing the big picture window in its frame and warping our reflections. The back of Lucas's head appeared to flare and narrow as he spoke.

"I miss them sorely," he said. "It's on and off, though. Sometimes I forget I even have kids. But just because I forget them doesn't mean they're not out there somewhere. You don't have to see your children to love them." He fingered the hunting knife, turned it over, scraping off the rust. "There would have been a third child, too, but my ex-wife took care of that. Showed up one day in divorce court two pounds lighter. Brand-new hairdo, too. A brutal woman."

He brandished the knife.

"Come here. I'm serious."

Kim took a half-step forward. One of her legs was shaking, wobbling at the knee. Another two steps and she would be between us, blocking Lucas's view of me.

She halted. "No."

The leg stopped shaking.

"No," she repeated. "You can come to me."

The laugh lines near Lucas's eyes went dark and crinkly. "Such a little firecracker. Mercy. What hath Ms. Gloria Steinem wrought?" He leaned forward in the chair and extended his left hand, taking hold of Kim's right hand. He held it by the wrist, palm up, like a fortune-teller.

Kim did not resist.

"You know what bothers me, Agnes? Secrecy. The sneakiness of women. Your murders are always committed in private. Some clinic. Some back alley. In the bathtub. You can't just come right out and do it. In public. You can't just perform an honest human sacrifice."

I decided to give reason one last try. "Lucas, you said you'd go when Kim made tea. Leave her alone now."

"The tea was shit."

He touched the knob on the side of the recliner. The chair straightened up, and so did the knife. The blade tip was maybe eight inches from Kim's belly. "Let's do this out in the open, for once. Full disclosure. So the men can see."

Keeping the knife pointed up, he released Kim's hand and reached under the chair and dragged out the red hot-water bottle with its coiled plastic hose. The bottle bulged with liquid. I got an acrid whiff of Lysol. "Of course, you can use a coat hanger instead—maybe you're a traditionalist. Either way, it's the same to me," said Lucas. "The point is honesty."

His eyes were fixed on Kim as I inched the paring knife out of my pocket and moved it behind my back and tensed my legs. I had a clear shot at his neck—I'd have to fly, though. He would see me, turn, and Kim could break away then—just as I started stabbing, hacking, carving. One unbroken motion, no stopping once it started. Let a judge and a jury sort it out.

My weight was all on the balls of my feet when Kim said to Lucas, "I think you had better just rape me instead." She undid a button, then another one, exposing the pale, freckled fronts of her thighs. Swaying and tipping on the high-heel shoes like a suicide on a windy building-ledge, she continued unbuttoning buttons until the whole gown was open. Naked breasts.

Lucas frowned and did not move. I sensed his confusion. It was time to act.

Kim wheeled and faced me. "Stay right there. I can take care of myself. I told you that."

Lucas cranked his neck around. He must have seen the small curved blade peeking from my fist, but not known what it was. He narrowed his eyes, looking puzzled.

I lunged.

Kim saw me coming—she blocked me with her fists raised. She pummeled my face and shoulders; I fell backward. The paring knife flew from my hand. I was down. Kim's mouth was open as she fell on top of me, but she didn't scream. She just kept hitting. I lay still and took it. Her fists were sharp and compact, like ball peen hammers. The beating seemed to go on for ages, and I could hear Lucas laughing in the background. Resonant, rich belly laughs. I told Kim to stop, that she was hurting me. Lucas laughed louder. I grabbed Kim's wrists. I felt the tension humming in her forearms, the voltage of her rage. I flashed on the scene in front of the clinic, when I had first laid hands on her and dragged her from harm's way. I had employed the same wrist-hold that morning.

A different situation, but the same hold.

"Let me go!" Kim yelled. "Let go of me!" Her tears were

amazing. So many, so hot. Where they hit my forehead it felt like blisters forming. She was whipping her hair around, struggling. A dervish. "I don't need a fucking savior," she shrieked. "Everyone just let me—"

Her brother was the one who pulled her off me. I wouldn't have thought Ricky capable of it, but suddenly there he was: stoned, uncomprehending, bruised, but moved by some primitive sibling instinct. He yanked Kim to her feet, then scolded her in that weird, loud voice of people who can't hear themselves, "Cut it out. You're nuts. Stop acting nuts."

I watched Kim shake herself free of Ricky's grasp and stumble to the bedroom door. She closed it behind her. I heard the latch click.

Everyone was quiet for a moment. Then Lucas rose from the rocker-recliner and sheathed the knife in the tooled-leather case hanging from his belt. He nodded at the front door, a gesture Ricky took as a command. He crossed the room and let himself out—a robot again, a follower. I thought I could hear him retching on the porch steps.

I sat up. I couldn't get a breath. My ribs were sore where Kim had pounded them.

Lucas said, "Theater. Fabulous theater. Boy meets she-bitch. Priceless."

"You get out."

"Gladly," Lucas said. "Can't top that act. Wouldn't even try. Just priceless . . ."

He turned and left the house.

I followed him to the door and locked the dead bolt. Through the picture window, I watched him lead poor Ricky to the station wagon. Lucas climbed in on the driver's side and there was a puff of exhaust from the tailpipe. He backed down the driveway and entered the road. He stopped for a moment, as though unsure of something, then turned the car toward the west and drove away.

I latched all the windows, for safety's sake, then went to the bedroom door and knocked.

Kim's voice said, "Go away."

"Please let me in."

Kim didn't answer.

"Open the door."

Silence.

"Are you okay, Kim?"

Like talking to a wall.

Exactly like that.

I gave up and sat down on the sofa. There was a phone on the side table. I dialed 911. A lady dispatcher answered, but I didn't know how to describe what had happened or what the relevant crime was. I hung up. I sat there for maybe ten minutes, blank, before seeing Ricky's joint on the floor. I found a lighter between the sofa cushions and lit the joint and inhaled. No effect. The bubble didn't form. Either it had burst for good or it had grown as large as the whole world.

Then I remembered something: an 800 number. To call when you needed help. A lifeline.

"Hello?" a voice said.

"Reverend Dale?"

"It's Dominic, his screener. Reverend Dale is not on the air yet, but if you can hold for fifteen minutes, sir . . ."

"I don't want to talk on the air," I said. "This is a personal call. Is he there?"

"This line is reserved for on-air problems only. If you'd like to contact the reverend personally, I can give you the address of his ministry and you can expect a reply within four weeks. Do you have a pencil handy?"

"No."

I hung up again.

I paced the floor for about an hour, pausing every few minutes to press my ear against the bedroom door. Nothing. Not a sound. There was only one thing I could think of to do—everything else had been tried.

I picked up the telephone one more time and dialed my mother the businesswoman.

Twenty-three

My mother's house was as large as I remembered. Hidden floodlights lit the yard, a burglar's obstacle course of dense rectangular hedges, goldfish ponds, and spiky wrought-iron fence. The royal-blue Lincoln Town Car parked in the semicircular drive had an official, diplomatic look, as though a flag belonged on the antenna. The sign above the front door that used to read THE WALQUISTS had been shortened to WALQUIST.

The door was unlocked.

"Make yourselves comfortable. See you in the morning."

My mother's voice came from up high and far away, pinning my feet to the welcome mat. The smell of the place was no smell, the odorlessness of immaculate habits. I wiped my feet on the mat and looked at Kim. She seemed transfixed by the sectional sofa that snaked through the sunken living room. Thirty feet of black Italian leather wrapped around a free-form coffee table hewn from a solid block of green marble. A jigsaw puzzle of the Parthenon missing only some sections of sky lay on the table's surface.

Kim said, "You grew up here?"

"Mmm. I tried."

I put her in the guest room. I unpacked my gym bag on my old bed, which had been left undisturbed since I moved away. An ancient stuffed rhinoceros with frayed cotton hide and button eyes that had come loose and hung by threads sat propped against the headboard. Model airplanes swooped down from the ceiling, nose cannons strafing the pillows. The only changed thing about the room was the snapshot collection tucked into my mirror frame. Arranged in order of age, the grainy Polaroids traced my life from uncertain first steps through smiling early school days through frowning teenage confusion. The last one showed me at my high-school prom, red-eyed and stoned, in a lavender tux. Before I went to bed, I hid the snapshots in a dresser drawer under a layer of old report cards, comic books, and clip-on neckties.

Once I'd undressed and lain down, I noticed a depression in the mattress where I guessed my mother had sat and viewed the Polaroids. It was unlike her to live in the past—I wondered if she'd changed. I decided to put the snapshots in an album and give it to her as a birthday present.

I could not sleep that night. After the long, silent drive from North Dakota, with Kim sitting frozen on the seat beside me like a sedated kidnapping victim, my head

ached and my thoughts would not shut up. The grand-
father clock downstairs chimed four A.M. as Kim left her
bedroom and padded down the hallway, past my open
door. A toilet flushed and Kim walked back. I didn't say
a word to her, just lay still and let her pass, the way I
should have done all along. My attempts to influence her
life had left us in a strange and sad position; I hoped my
mother could turn things around. Maybe her practical
attitude, her faith in schedules and experts and the power
of well-spent money was just the thing we needed now.

The next morning was hard. While Kim was still in bed,
I sat at the kitchen table with my mother and filled in the
story I'd told her on the phone. It was the whole story,
minus certain fiendish details. Listening, sipping a Slim
Fast shake, surrounded by banks of restaurant-grade appliances that had never been used to prepare a single
meal, my mother seemed sympathetic but bored, as
though I were exaggerating problems she and her friends
had faced a hundred times. Several times she cut me off
and told me to get to the point, which for her seemed to
be Kim's state of mind—her goals and her desires. "But
what does she *want*?" my mother kept asking. I said I
wasn't sure. Finally, I described Kim's greeting cards.

My mother said only, "Do they sell?"

I said yes, a few had sold.

"She should stick with it, then. Persistence pays."

"The cards aren't that good, though."

"Regardless."

My mother also pressed me to talk about myself, but
once again she grew impatient, insisting that I give her
lines, not colors; statements, not descriptions. She made
me feel that all the time I had spent apart from her equaled
a sort of extended shore leave. A holiday. A gap. Now

that I was home, however, my real life could resume—
that was my mother's drift. She promised to buy me a
new, sharper wardrobe. She offered me a job.

"I don't want to work in a liquor store," I said.

"You mean you just don't want to work."

"Let's drop it, Margaret. We're here because of Kim, not
me. I can take care of myself."

"And so can she, no doubt," my mother said. "But never
mind. I understand. You'd like me to talk to the girl
immediately?"

"That's why we came all this way."

My mother reached across the table and laid a hand on
one of mine. "Then do the women a favor. Go somewhere.
Leave us alone for the day. To talk."

I looked at her age-spotted hand. It appeared to have
shrunk since I had seen it last. Rings that were once pro-
portioned to her fingers seemed outlandish now, like
Christmas ornaments.

"Fine. I'll go to the movies," I said.

My mother gave me a bill from her purse. I put the bill
in my wallet, a reflex. A reflex it was time I overcame.

I laid the bill on the table. "I can pay for my own movie.
Thanks."

"Baloney. You're broke," my mother said. "You and
your whole generation. But soon I'll die and you'll be rich
as me. Here—" She opened her purse again, which was
stuffed with cash. "Consider it an advance on your inheri-
tance."

It was too early for so much perspective. I stuffed my
mother's money in my jeans and hoped she would lighten
up a bit before she spoke to Kim.

I did not see a movie that day. After Kim woke up, after
the slightly awkward introductions, after my mother and

Kim sat down to breakfast, I drove for about a mile, parked my car on the shoulder of the road, then hiked cross-country through woods and backyards until I was back within sight of the house. I sat on the ground and ants crawled over me. I watched the house for a sign.

A decision was being made in there; I deserved to be present, if only from a distance.

Two or three hours later, I saw them. First, my mother, carrying two suitcases. She set them down next to her Lincoln, then went back into the house. She reappeared with Kim, who was lugging a couple bags of her own. My mother opened the Lincoln's trunk and together the women stowed their bags, working like a team. My mother slammed the trunk lid and she and Kim hugged each other. For a moment, it looked as if they were going to part. But no, it was just a hug of affection. My mother opened the car door for Kim, then walked around to the driver's side.

Running, I could have been there in a minute. Or I could have yelled for them to stop. Instead, I lay down on the ground and spread my arms out. I heard my mother's car start. Ants marched in columns across my neck and chest, refusing to let me divert their supply lines. I heard the Lincoln drive off. I watched the ants.

They climbed right over me, big black ants, behaving as though I weren't even there.

Three days later, when Kim returned, I was out of the house, in town, lining up a job as a sales rep for Northco Industrial Cleaning Supplies. The interviewer seemed to like me. He assured me his firm was nothing like Sani-pure; Northco's products, he said, were all high quality, and environmentally friendly to boot. He made quite a speech on the subject, even suggesting that Northco's soaps and solvents actually *improved* our air and water. I accepted the job, but with a stipulation: that I would not have to lie to customers about some detergent saving the world. I had had enough of that.

Driving home, I stopped at a florist and picked up a modest bouquet of tulips. I paid for it out of the two thousand dollars my mother had left on the marble coffee table the day she went away with Kim. There was a note on the table telling me when to expect them back and what I should do in the meantime: have the cleaning lady in, order a larger bed for my room, and install softer bulbs in the light fixtures there. My mother also suggested renting several movies ("Popcorn stuff," she wrote. "Nothing dark or morbid") to have on hand for Kim's return. I had carried out these instructions precisely, dwelling as little as possible on their implications. I had asked my mother to take charge, and that is what she'd done—I'd expected nothing less of her. The only thing in her note that surprised me was her failure to list specific movie titles.

Kim was on the couch when I came in, lying facedown on a heating pad and watching the big-screen TV. I put the tulips on top of the set. At first, I couldn't look Kim in the eye. I fiddled with the flowers, making them all the same length, and asked her how she was feeling.

She said, "Crampy."

The word took my breath away.

When I recovered, I said, "Where's my mother?"

"Upstairs somewhere. She's tired from driving."

I asked Kim if she needed anything. She held out an empty water glass.

"You can mix some Kool-Aid. The doctor said I need to raise my blood sugar."

I took the glass. "The doctor."

Kim rolled on her side and looked at me. "We went to Chicago. A clinic there. Your mother was great. She really was. I owe her."

I nodded and looked away, at the TV. The movie was one I had rented: *E.T.: The Extraterrestrial*. I had never seen it, but I knew its reputation for inspiring warm, cozy feelings in children. Indeed, it occurred to me then that all the movies I'd rented were for children. I hadn't planned it that way. It just happened.

"I'll mix up that Kool-Aid," I said.

We didn't go to bed that night. We watched the movies, one after the other, mechanically putting popcorn in our mouths and swallowing glass after glass of sweet red punch. Kim didn't seem to mind, or even notice, that all the movies were rated G. We saw *Swiss Family Robinson*, *Mary Poppins*, something called *The Goonies*, and one of my all-time favorites, *Jason and the Argonauts*. We sat there as though fulfilling some strange sentence, some order a judge had handed down. We might as well have been handcuffed to our chairs.

Every hour or so, I asked a question.

"Did it hurt?"

"A lot. Incredibly."

"You decided the other morning? Or when?"

"You don't decide. You know."

"Maybe you'd like to go to church on Sunday?"

"Sunday is four days away. Let's watch the movie."

Television, Kool-Aid, fragments of conversation. That's how it was for us those next few days. For me, on Sunday, church. For Kim, sitting up in our new queen-size bed, putting thoughts for new cards onto paper. Me, I had no thoughts. They stopped. They stopped for a couple of weeks. And when they slowly started up again, one of them was, "We're damned now. Kim especially," and another was, "We're fine," and sometimes, "I have to get out of this house," and other times, "It died so we could live."

More and more thoughts every day, until individual thoughts mattered less than the patterns made by sets of thoughts, and then there were so many sets of thoughts that I could no longer keep track of them and it was a lot like normal life again.

What Kim's thoughts were I can't pretend to know, although I suspect her experience was different—a narrowing down from many thoughts to one thought.

She said it sometimes after sex, in the dark: "I can still be a mother someday."

I could keep going from there. From the thoughts of a few weeks afterward to how Kim is doing and how I am doing to what my mother and Kim discussed that morning to whether I've even continued to see Kim, but those are private matters. Now I see that. Strangers deserve to know only so much, and I have already revealed more than I should have.

So until we all sit down together and tell all our secrets and prayers all at once, no bluffing or holding back or making someone else go first, and all our bubbles burst into one, I am stopping here.

Because it's private.